GOING FOR BROKE

T. G. Horne was definitely on a roll.

First he had won a gambling hall in the wildest poker hand he had ever played.

Then he had found the perfect staff for it when he recruited a lovely local Madame and her string of seductive sirens.

And now the most stunning of the whole curvacious crew had invited Horne up to her room. Her name was Star and one thing became very clear as she stripped off her dress. This particular piece of luck was no lady—but Horne was ready to play it to its limit. . . .

THE COCKEYED COYOTE

PIERCE MacKENZIE

(I)
A SIGNET BOOK
NEW AMERICAN LIBRARY

PUBLISHER'S NOTE

This book is a work of fiction. Names, characters, places, and incidents either are the product of the author's imagination or are used fictitiously, and any resemblance to actual persons, living or dead, events, or locales is entirely coincidental.

SIGNET TRADEMARK REG. U.S. PAT. OFF. AND FOREIGN COUNTRIES
REGISTERED TRADEMARK—MARCA REGISTRADA
HECHO EN CHICAGO, U.S.A.

SIGNET, SIGNET CLASSIC, MENTOR, ONYX, PLUME, MERIDIAN and NAL BOOKS are published by NAL PENGUIN INC., 1633 Broadway, New York, New York 10019

First Printing, October, 1987

1 2 3 4 5 6 7 8 9

PRINTED IN THE UNITED STATES OF AMERICA

Pericles Jubal Youngquist drew back from the knothole in the side of the boxcar and turned to address his traveling companion. "I make it about five miles to Muddy Springs from here. We don't want to get off in town, do we? Not me, not looking and smelling like this."

T. G. Horne, sitting at the front of the otherwise empty car, his back to the wall, forearms balanced on his knees, shoulders slumped, spirits as flat as his wallet, sighed and nodded. "I suppose."

"Then get up and help me open the door."

The train had started up a grade and was slowing, creaking and groaning like a mythical monster in pain. The whistle hooted, the engine chuffed and slowed further.

"Move!" barked Perry.

Together they slid the heavy door open just enough to slip through. Horne jumped first, landing, his left leg buckling, toppling him hard to the gravel, triggering a string of curses. Quickly he regained his feet, ran alongside the train, and caught Perry as he jumped. Or rather, he tried to catch him; Perry's weight knocked him down a second time. Uncle helped nephew to his feet. They stood watching the train lumber up the steepening incline, then turned and studied each other. They were as black as the night surrounding them: heads, faces, hands, every exposed inch of their flesh. Both were hatless; wisps of feathers clung to their tar; their darkened faces made their eyes look as large and white as billiard balls. Horne resumed picking the feathers from his scalp and forehead.

"Tarred, feathered, ridden out of town on a rail," groused Perry. "I've never been so humiliated in my entire life. It's so degrading, so base. Villainous rascals! Odious scoundrels!"

"What are you blaming them for? They caught you cheating red-handed; what do you expect, a medal? We're lucky they didn't string us up. I was a fool for coming to your defense."

"Only a craven poltroon wouldn't have."

"I did, didn't I? Why, God only knows; dropping two aces out of your sleeve smack in the middle of the table. Of all the stupid, totally moronic—"

"It was an accident!"

"Beautifully timed, flawlessly executed. Stand still. Where do you think you're going? Before we go anywhere, shouldn't we figure our next move? Ridding ourselves of this tar and feathers might do for starters. Dear Lord but you stink!"

"You're not exactly an armful of roses yourself, my boy."

Perry scanned the landscape. About a mile from the tracks squatted a small farm, house, barn, and woodshed black against the blue-black sky. A light glowed in a front window.

"What time is it?" Perry asked.

Horne shrugged. "How would I know? The bastards stole my watch."

Perry surveyed the star-strewn heavens. "It can't be much past ten o'clock. They ran us out of Hooksville around nine, according to the clock in the jewelry-store window across the street from Haggerty's. We weren't on the train more than an hour. Let's head for that spread. When we get there, I'll do the talking."

"Only if whoever opens the door stops laughing long enough to let you."

"I see nothing funny about this," Perry snapped.

"Neither do I, but we have to think about the rest of the world." They started off. "You mind telling me something? Why were you holding out those aces anyway?

There wasn't an experienced player at that table, and not one any luckier than either of us. Why cheat when there's no need to?"

"One can never tell when the need will arise. I was thinking ahead. I didn't hold them long, just for a couple hands. We'd been playing better than an hour, a big pot was due to show. Great Caesar's ghost, that tar was hot going on; it feels like it's burned away my top layer of skin. I dread removing it."

"Then leave it on. Quit gambling and get yourself a job with a minstrel troupe."

Perry gave neither verbal response nor expression of disapproval to this. Instead, he bowed his white-maned head and trudged wearily off toward the light. Horne followed. Tarred and feathered, he mused; over the years gambling about the territories they'd come close to getting their heads blown off on more occasions than he cared to recall, but tar, feathers, and a rail were a new experience, and a decidedly unpleasant one. Whoever originally conceived such a treatment for flimflam and bunco artists and other undesirable visitors must have had a singularly diabolical mind. To combine so much pain with so much humor was ingenious. The tar hurt, the feathers were comically ignominious—he could still hear the laughter; the ride on the rail, the landing in the ditch outside of town appropriately uncomfortable, painful, and mortifying. Still, all of it was preferable to being shot or lynched. The other players were certainly angry enough to kill them; it was the kibitzers who came up with the alternate punishment and relieved them of their money, watches, and Horne's weapons and treasured diamond horseshoe stickpin. They'd been lucky to get their clothes back, all but their hats.

What a night, what a debacle—all because Perry thoughtlessly dropped his right arm when he should have kept it raised. Gravity was the culprit. The two aces appearing struck terror into his heart. All conversation had ceased immediately, as if turned off by a master switch. The icy silence that followed hung over the table like a guillotine blade. Perry, who had risen from his chair to better assess the pot, stood frozen. Someone cursed, someone else accused, then six pair of strong hands seized Perry. Horne jumped to his defense. Six more pair of hands seized him. The next thing either of them knew, they were standing stripped to their underwear over a cutaway half of a fifty-gallon barrel filled with simmering, ominously bubbling tar. Three feather pillows were brought up, ripped open, and the fun began. Everyone in the game took part, passing the tar brush around, flinging feathers.

Perry was right, so hot was the tar going on it had to have burned away the outer layer of skin; removing the tar would surely make the tortures of the ancients seem like a sitz bath in comparison.

They were now within twenty feet of the front door. Rambler roses crowded trellises at either side of it. There was no veranda; the house was crudely built, but freshly painted a pristine white. Inside, music could be faintly heard. Horne recognized "Virginia Skedaddle," punctuated by the thumping of clog dancing and occasional merry shouting. It was one of the more-spirited popular plantation songs recorded for the victrola. Sure goes well with tar and feathers, he thought.

"Remember," said Perry, "I'll do the talking."

He knocked. The door opened immediately, as if the woman who'd opened it was standing on the other side with her hand on the knob. She was middle-aged, buxom, determinedly maternal-looking, her graying brown hair done up for the night in a host of paper curlers that looked like marooned butterflies. She wore spectacles that had descended her nose to within a quarter-inch of the tip. She held an embroidery ring and needle; she was chewing tobacco; she took one look and burst out laughing.

"Land o' Goshen, mercy me! [Laughter] Aren't you boys a little early for Halloween? [Laughter] Or are you with the New Christy minstrels? [Laughter] If you don't look ridiculous! [Laughter] Hilarious!"

"Permit me to introduce us," said Perry huffily. "Benjamin Marblehall, Esquire. This is Mr. Alistair Richardson, my traveling companion."

"Mary Alice Tubbs, two b's. Come in, come in." She

paused and let fly tobacco juice in a short brown arc between them. "Excuse. Oh, my stars, this is a down home riot! [Laughter] I haven't seen tar and feathers since I was nine. What did you do, get caught cheating in a poker game?"

"It was a horrendous mistake," said Perry evenly. "A misunderstanding the size of your barn."

"It was no misunderstanding," interposed Horne. "Mr. Marblehall here accidentally dropped two aces out of his sleeve. From that point on, it was all downhill."

"Do tell." She had brought her face right up to Perry's, peering at him over her glasses. "If you don't look like enough to scare the chickens into holding tight. How'd you get your clothes back?"

"Two of our attackers turned out to be slightly less flint-hearted than the others. Dear lady, would you by chance have a plunge bath and some glycerine or something?"

"What you want is kerosene. There's a tin out in the woodshed. Al, you go get it. You, Ben, into the guest room and strip. I'll fetch the plunge bath."

The hot tar going on had been sheer torture; removing it with the kerosene was even worse. Horne's whole body felt like a single, outsized, all-encompassing hornet sting. Were he to close his eyes, he would have sworn he was on fire from head to toe. Every inch of flesh glowed an angry red; every hair, but for those on his scalp, his eyebrows, and pubic hair, was wrenched from its mooring. In such agony was he throughout the first half-hour after emerging from his kerosene bath, he could only stand naked dancing from one leg to the other, puffing like an elephant seal, the tears running down his rosy cheeks. At the end of that time the pain began to abate; either that or he became used to it and he was able to get back into his underwear. All he craved at this point was bed and a bottle to empty, something powerful enough to stupify him so that he might sleep away the next three days.

His own escape from the tar and feathers to some degree restored Perry's dignity. It was a quarter to twelve by the fancy gilt-bronze basket Waterbury clock with the three carved kittens cavorting around it when uncle and nephew, fully clad, rejoined their Good Samaritan in her parlor.

"Feeling better?" she asked. She had walked to the open window, ejecting her chaw into the night. "Excuse."

Perry nodded. "Immensely, dear lady. We're indebted to you for life."

"Aces up your sleeve was it? Isn't that risky? Wouldn't it have been safer to palm them out and shove them under your rear end? You must have been up against some real sharks to take such a desperate chance." Horne and Perry exchanged glances. "Oh, I know something about cards; my late husband was a gambling man. Not especially good at it, but he tried. Poker mostly. I was glad when he quit. Became a federal marshal. I still have his badge. Dangerous work, but not as bad as sneaking aces up your sleeve. Isn't that kind of old-fashioned as well as dangerous?"

"Definitely," said Horne. Perry glared at him but said not a word.

"Well, it's not for me to criticize; the two of you look like you paid through the nose for this night's doings. You're welcome to a free bed and board for tonight if you want it. Hungry?"

Horne's pathetic sigh was all the answer she needed. She trotted out three-quarters of a leg of lamb, fresh parsnips, green beans, and potatoes. Both ate ravenously. Mrs. Tubbs put another record on the victrola: Issher's orchestra performing selections from *Erminie*. The music floated prettily through the room.

"Where'bouts you bound for?" she asked.

"Nowhere in particular," said Horne.

"Muddy Springs is just up the road, isn't it?" Perry asked.

"Next train stop. Nothing much there. Couple saloons, a dance hall. It's a town that should be bigger than it is, it being the first stop over the border on the Chisholm Trail. Before Caldwell. But for some reason it never has taken 'vantage of that. Fewer than two hundred folks live there. I expect you're both tapped out."

Perry nodded. "Clean as a whistle."

"Both of you were playing?"

"I was in and out," said Horne. "I was kibitzing when disaster struck. Actually, just taking a break."

"We were both just about holding our own," added Perry. "The opposition was no great shakes, but they seemed to have a corner on the luck."

"So you decided to do something about it." She turned to Horne. "And when he got caught you had to stick your two cents in." She cocked her head and eyed him so critically it caused him to shrink his head slightly deeper between his shoulders.

Horne scowled. "They already knew we were partners. We sat down together."

"That was brilliant. Sounds to me like you were careless every step of the way. What are you going to do for money after you leave here?"

Perry finished eating, licked his thumbs, applied his napkin to his greasy mouth, wiped his hands, sighed satisfaction, patted his lean paunch, and tried to smile through his discomfort. "Rob a bank?"

"I hope you're better at that. Seriously, I could lend you. Stake you to a game. You," she added, turning her glance to Horne again. "Not you, Ben. I'm assuming you don't cache cards up your sleeve. Are you any good?"

"Mrs. Tubbs, Mary Alice, you are looking at the premier poker player of the West. It's no exaggeration to say that Mr. Richardson here is without question the top earner on the circuit."

"Who at that moment is flat. Let's see how good you are, Al."

She cleared the side table, set it in the center of the parlor, got out a well-used pack of Dougherty's Climax Number 14 cards and a set of chips, distributed the chips among the three of them, shuffled expertly, and dealt draw.

"Jacks or better to open. Progressive."

Perry's queens opened. They played until one o'clock. Horne, with no small amount of clever and expertly concealed assistance from Perry, won everything but the table. His performance satisfied Mary Alice Tubbs.

"I'll advance you two hundred. If you lose it, forget it. If you win, I'll take double my money back. There are some fair country poker players in Muddy Springs. Watch out for Amos Darling; he cheats and he's good at it. Particularly good at palming discards. Left-handed and never uses his sleeve. Watch out for Byron Culkin, the banker's son. He's lucky as hell, very patient and with a memory like a six-pound magnet. Watch out for Hugh Toricelli; give him half a chance and he'll slip readers in on you; he leans toward belly-strippers. Keep your eyes and ears open, wait for the breaks, bet 'em when you get 'em, and keep both sleeves clear. Boys, it's late, I'm tired, I'm going to bed. You'll find clean towels by your washstand. Al, you can put away the plunge bath; it goes out in the barn. Hangs from a nail just inside the door. And put back what's left of the kerosene while you're at it. In the woodshed. Sleep well, boys. Fresh eggs, bacon, home-made bread and jam, and Arbuckle's for breakfast."

2

The Cockeyed Coyote Saloon in Muddy Springs could have used a thorough sweeping and dusting before being hosed down. A line of vertical slats reaching belt buckle high and capped by molding covered the lower portions of the walls. Wallpaper in faded maroon and yellow in a nondescript pattern ascended to the gambrel ceiling. Adorning the upper walls were stag and moose heads, a stuffed cougar on a shelf over the rear door, two stuffed mallards, a stuffed, one-eyed, and sadly deteriorated wolf. There were portraits and landscapes in cracked and flaking gilded frames. The bar was long but uncommonly narrow, and no odalisque reclined at her ease above the mirror in the rear. Spittoons and roundback chairs surrounded rickity tables. But the decorator's pièce de résistance remained outside, a four-times-as-large-as-life carved wooden coyote head mounted on a wooden replica of an Indian's war shield above the swinging doors. It gazed down cross-eyed through orbs the size of billard balls.

Upon entering, Perry took one look and assumed the pained expression he generally reserved for minor disappointments.

"This place doesn't need tidying, it needs a fire."

"Ssssh."

The gathering of patrons was orderly, the single bartender busy dispensing drinks. Perry and Horne approached him and inquired about the game. The man, burly and blond, his hair parted dead-center and so securely plas-

13

tered to his pate it looked sculptured, nodded toward the
rear door. The drop octogon clock fixed to the mirror
behind him read 8:09.

"Boys is in there. Ain't started yet. Go on in and interduce
yourselves. What's yer pleasure?" He swiped the mahogany in front of them with a rag that smelled of seventeen
different brands.

"Would you by chance stock a halfway decent imported
brandy?" asked Perry.

"You betcha, imported all the way from Callyfornya."

Perry's pained look returned momentarily as he nodded. Horne ordered whiskey, sipped a third of it and paid
for it all. Then he and Perry, with his Sonoma Valley
brandy, sauntered to the rear, the two of them running a
gauntlet of curious stares from the locals. The rear door
opened onto a room half again the size of the bar proper.
There was ample space for a dozen poker games, but only
one table was visible, bare and surrounded by seven chairs.
Three were occupied.

Amos Darling, whom Mary Alice Tubbs had warned
them cheated, was in his fifties, a strikingly handsome,
rapid talking, nattily attired individual sporting an elk's
tooth and a ring with a diamond the size of a wren's egg.
The sight of it actuated a nostalgic tug at Horne's heart as
he thought of his own lost diamond stickpin. Darling
introduced himself, Byron Culkin and Hugh Toricelli.
Culkin, the best player of the three—at least the luckiest
in Mary Alice's opinion—was half Darling's age. He looked
to Horne like an albino, his pink eyes fringed with pure
white lashes, his skin deathly pale. From the cuffs of his
jacket hung the longest, slenderest hands he had ever
seen, hands custom designed by Nature to handle cards
dexterously, efficiently—dishonestly? No, Mary Alice had
characterized him as the lucky, patient one with the fox
trap memory. Hugh Toricelli looked like he weighed 250
pounds, and without an ounce of fat on his frame—as
slim-waisted as Perry, with a chest and shoulders capable
of collapsing a barn by the simple expedient of inhaling
against it. Any man that big and strong would have few
qualms about cheating at poker or anything else; few of his

average opponents would be so foolhardy as to accuse him. He did make Horne wonder, however; all three were locals, they must play together frequently, perhaps all the time. How did the others put up with Toricelli's cheating? Why continue playing with him? Or did he play crookedly only against strangers?

Whatever the case, the three of them warranted close watching. He was grateful to Mary Alice for warning them, but of course she was only protecting her investment. The night before in her little lecture delivered just before they retired, T.G. hadn't needed her advice to keep his eyes and ears open. Indeed, he'd been mildly insulted that she should think either he or Perry needed it. Still, let her say what she pleased, it was her money. The thought of it sent his hand down into his pocket where it lay folded, warm and ready to go to work.

Ten minutes later, in trooped nine men of varying ages, sizes, and conditions: at least two quite drunk, in spite of the early hour. Two took chairs at the table; the rest sat and stood prepared to kibitz. The bartender, whose name was Roy, pronounced "Raw" by some of the kibitzers, provided a new deck of Tally-ho's wrapped in plain brown paper in their box, and chips. The chips were purchased, the bank double-checked, the cards dealt. The first jack that appeared fell to Perry, whom Horne had armed with fifty dollars of Mary Alice's money. He began with five-card draw, nothing wild, jacks or better to open.

Horne spent the first hour concentrating intently on their opposition. Amos Darling and Byron Culkin ran true to the form described by Mary Alice. Hugh Toricelli had not yet tried to sneak belly-strippers, pricked cards, or any other type of readers into the game. Whether he planned to was questionable, but the night was still young. His style of play interested Horne. It was discouragingly prevalent among amateurs. He swung back and forth like a pendulum between plunging and conservative play. When he plunged and lost, he invariably pulled in his horns and played the next few hands tightly. It almost seemed that his courage, deflated by losing, had to be recharged before he could again wield it. He was the poorest player of the

three. The other two players had come in with the troupe
of kibitzers: one, Moses Oblowicz, was the managing partner of the local dry-goods store, and the oldest man at the
table, exceeding Perry by a good five years, was afflicted
with palsy. His hands shook so when he dealt Horne
marveled that the cards did not spill and flip and fly in
every direction. But despite his age and affliction, he had
a keen mind and memory for discards, and obvious vast
experience in the game. He won steadily if not spectacu-
larly playing intelligently, dropping out at precisely the
right time, something Hugh Toricelli had either no talent
for or no interest in doing.

The seventh player called himself Bill and was a wheat
farmer whose spread neighbored Mary Alice Tubbs' land.
From the conversation, Horne gathered that he only came
to town to play every other week, while the other four
assembled every other night, excepting Sundays. Horne
could understand why Bill played infrequently. He was
without question one of the poorest poker players he'd
ever run into. In draw he could not seem to make up his
mind what to hold, what to discard. Time and again the
others had to wait patiently for him to decide, and invariably when he did, it turned out the wrong decision. In five-
and seven-card stud he either stayed too long or dropped
out too early. He had no memory for the cards, wouldn't
have dreamed of evaluating his hand in terms of the pot,
pulled to inside straights, ignored and defied the odds,
and broke almost every other basic rule of the game. Over
the course of the first two hours of play he won but one
hand, and that by default, when his opponent carelessly
misread his own hand, staying with a pair of sixes, admit-
ting in the end that he thought he held three. He was the
only one at the table drinking, which helped neither his
vision nor thinking. Bill dropped out shortly after ten,
lamenting his "rotten luck," saying nothing whatsoever
about his "rotten play." His chair was commandeered by a
tall, red-haired man introduced as Albert Cutshaw. He
was the owner of the Cockeyed Coyote, just returned
from Wellington after a four-day business trip.

"I rode like blue blazes to get back here by eight, but

wouldn't you know the bridge over the Chikaskia was out and I had to detour clear up to Argonia to get across."

Horne and Perry were introduced, and the game continued. As sometimes happens in poker, usually late in the evening, two of the group will begin to bump heads. So it was to be with Horne and Cutshaw.

Cutshaw liked to bluff: semi-bluffs, that is a bet made with more cards to come which, if called, is probably not the best hand at the moment but has a reasonable chance of becoming the best hand and pure bluff—a bet that, if called, has no chance of winning in a showdown.

Horne prided himself on being able to spot a bluff a desert mile away. Cutshaw nevertheless beat him, semi-bluffing him in no fewer than three hands. With luck, to be sure, outdrawing him at the end of each of them. It was almost 11:30 and they'd agreed on a 1:00 A.M. curfew. Horne was many thousands to the good, Perry about three hundred. There was plenty of time to catch up with Cutshaw and skin him out of one or two outsized pots, so Horne wasn't worried. But he had to concede, however grudgingly, that Cutshaw was one of the better, albeit luckier bluffers he'd ever come up against. On went the game. Horne reflected.

Vengeance is mine, he said to himself, if you don't mind me borrowing it, Lord. Losing the money didn't bother him. Thanks to a remarkable run of cards that streaked through a series of huge pots, he was up by some twenty thousand dollars.

Being bluffed and thrice beaten on the come was what irked.

It was nearing half-past twelve and the humiliating ordeal he and Perry had suffered the previous evening was beginning to tell on his energy, despite a fair night's sleep at the widow Tubbs'. His skin still stung and the remnants of a headache lingered. Perry called for draw, set the pack before Cutshaw, sitting to his right. Cutshaw cut, Perry dealt.

Horne fought to keep a poker face and his eyes from widening in the slightest as he picked up his five cards. Rarely did such a gem, a jewel of the Indies, come to hand. And when it does, when the light of luck flashing its beam about the room isolates you alone, exclusively, bathing you in its golden glow, generally just as rare is it to have other players stay in the hand and play against you. How frequent it is in every poker player's history to pull a spectacular hand, a one in precisely 72,194 hands, only to see everyone else fold early, in spite of your every clever effort to keep them in the game.

In his pink and suddenly slightly perspiring left hand were five cards in a combination that struck up a full orchestra in his soul, a chorus of angels in his heart. Hosts of violins blended beautifully, deep-throated brass horns intoned sonorously, reeds united their mellow voices, and altos and sopranos set his mind whirling dizzily in time to the glorious melody.

Hugh Toricelli, sitting on Perry's left, opened the betting, pushing twenty dollars in reds toward the pot. When it came round to Horne, he raised him twenty. To his surprise and elation, Amos Darling, sitting to his left, raised an additional fifty. To his astonishment, Byron Culkin called.

Three players staying with him! Would wonders never cease?

The betting arrived at Cutshaw. He raised a hundred dollars. Perry dropped, Culkin dropped out of turn. Toricelli reraised an additional five hundred. Horne sat with his cards facedown, their combination branded on the screen of his mind, each pip set with a gleaming diamond, each border trimmed with pure platinum. He briefly pondered his next move. He had the money, he could easily up the bet another five hundred dollars, but no, better to just call. Among all the raising and reraising, a call at this propitious juncture would stand out like a red flag in a field of ripe cotton. And send a clear message to everyone: "I'm good enough to stay, just not good enough to raise."

Perry was eyeing him. Horne avoided looking his way. Out of the corner of his eye, he could see the ends of his mouth turn slightly up, as if there was a smile behind his tightly sealed lips trying to get out.

"Six-fifty to you, Richardson," said Amos Darling.

"I'll call."

By now everyone else had folded, leaving only the four of them. The pot already approximated two thousand dollars, and they hadn't even drawn their cards yet. Perry, dealing, prepared to do so. The bet was to Toricelli.

"I'll play these," he said mildly. "I bet two thousand."

"I'll play these," said Horne mildly. "Make it five thousand."

Sudden panic seized Amos Darling's handsome face. His eyes darted about the table like those of a cornered fox. A decision was forming in his mind. He obviously didn't relish it, obviously despised it, but just as obviously could see no way to avoid it.

"I'm out."

He flung down his cards and sat scowling, his lips moving slightly, his eyes fixed on the pot.

"It's to you, Albert," said Toricelli.

"I'll play these," said Cutshaw mildly. "I'll see your five thousand and make it ten."

Low whistles and murmurs raced around the table. Horne craned his neck slightly to assess Cutshaw's chips. His mammoth bet had reduced his stacks to under a hundred dollars. Horne studied his own chips. He estimated them at just about twelve thousand dollars. Into the pot he nudged nine thousand, eliciting even louder, more surprised, dumbfounded comments from the onlookers.

Toricelli dropped. Unlike Amos Darling's folding, he did not appear to take it hard; he appeared too stunned. The expression on his dark face was that of a man who'd just been told he'd been wiped out and his wife had run off with his banker.

"I'll see your ten thousand and raise you four," said Horne.

Toricelli erupted from his shock. "Goddamn son-of-a-bitch bastard," he boomed, and flung his hand angrily to the table. Carelessly flipping his cards faceup, revealing four sevens. "Best goddamn fucking hand I've pulled all night and you, you . . . awwwww . . ."

Two players. Head to head. Cutshaw was dagger-eying Horne. For a seemingly interminable length of time no one spoke, no one moved so much as a finger, one and all: players and kibitzers alike barely breathed. The air in the room had become stifling. Horne was sweating profusely. The skin under his collar itched. A lump the size of a Belgin block had formed on the floor of his stomach. It began to ache, filling his stomach with cramps. His bowels felt as if they were loosening. His back teeth ached, his eyeballs burned.

He shifted them toward Perry. Perry's smile, previously concealed behind his lips, showed itself. He winked. Cutshaw continued moving his eyes from his chips to the pot to Horne's face and back to his chips.

"I'm just about tapped out . . ."

Horne let out a long breath, shrugged, lowered his cards, relaxed his poker face, and reached for the pot.

"Hold it, goddammit! What's the rush? I said tapped out, not dropped out."

"Then you call?"

"Damn tootin' I call!"

"With what?"

"With . . . with . . . Roy!" he shouted. "Open the goddamn door, somebody." The kibitzer nearest it did so. "Roy Pendleton, get in here. Pronto!"

The bartender materialized in the doorway, wiping his hands on his heavily stained apron, his expression questioning.

"There you are," burst Cutshaw. "Jesus Christ, it took you long enough. Open up the safe and get out the goddamn deed."

Horne stiffened. "Cutshaw . . ."

"Do like I tell ya, goddammit! Be quick about it!"

"Cutshaw," repeated Horne.

"You just shut up, I'm callin' you. Four thousand, right?"

"Four thousand."

"I'm callin'. You're not bluffin' me this time, I got you beat all hollow. My four thousand is the Coyote. I'm puttin' her up."

Everyone, even Perry, gasped. Everyone, except Horne. From the look on Cutshaw's face he seemed to think

Horne either hadn't heard him clearly or had failed to grasp his meaning.

"The Coyote, the Coyote! This place!" He swept his arms, encompassing the room. "The whole, entire works. Christ almighty, it's worth twice four thousand, maybe three times, but I don't give a shit. I won't lose it. I got the winning hand right here and I'll be goddamned and ridden to hell on a busted mule if I let you snatch this one out from under my nose. I got the winner, she's my pot, my money!"

He held up the deed with both hands for Horne to read.

"Signed, sealed, the genuine article. Legal as hell. Anybody in this room, anybody in Muddy Springs, in Sumner County'll attest to it. And it's worth twice what I'm puttin' it up for. The works: the bar, booze, furniture. That bar out front, in case you didn't notice, is one piece o' Filipino mahogany. Cost a goddamn pretty penny."

"Albert," began Horne softly, "with all due respect, I know you think you have the winning hand, I'll concede that paper is worth four thousand—"

"Eight! Double! I'm puttin' it up for four, only 'cause you got my back to the goddamn wall. But not for long. Mister, I got you beat to death!"

Horne's glance again moved to Perry. Perry's eyes had ceased twinkling; they looked as hard as two sapphires. Slowly, almost imperceptibly, he nodded. Horne answered it. A guttural sound issued from Cutshaw's throat. He looked on the verge of exploding, blowing himself into tiny bits of raw flesh and bone, spreading blood all over the room. Into the pot he flung the deed.

"Call!"

Horne cleared his throat. Everyone leaned forward. "Straight spade flush," he said quietly.

Silence struck. The silence of the tomb eerie, icy. No one moved. No one breathed.

"Oh . . . my . . . God," whispered Cutshaw hollowly.

In an instant all his bravado deserted him, his voice all but fled with it, reducing itself to a coarse, hoarse, barely audible gasping. To Horne, the air in his body seemed to issue from its apertures, deflating him like a punctured balloon. For a long second Horne worried that his heart would thump its last and over the table he would slump dead.

"Oh, my God," he repeated.

Horne had laid his hand down. Straight spade flush: eight to the queen. Cutshaw laid down his straight spade flush: deuce to the six.

Horne raked in the pot.

3

It was very late; Muddy Springs slept peacefully. Although a curfew of 1:00 A.M. had been put on the game, play ended with Horne's spectacular triumph. Players and kibitzers had fled into the night. A handful of patrons lingered at the bar. Horne and Perry stood outside under the wooden head of the saloon's namesake, Perry tugging thoughtfully on his stogie, Horne nursing the butt of a Jersey cheroot within an inch of its ash. A three-quarter moon sailed the cobalt sky directly above the Cockeyed Coyote, and a billion stars pulsed nervously and tirelessly. A breeze came up, setting up a dust dancer. It performed briefly, dissolved, and died. Perry launched a blue circle of smoke and chuckled softly.

"Unbelievable. Two spade flushes in the same hand. In fifty years I've never seen such a deal, not without wild cards. I've seen two royal flushes head to head. Straight flushes, too. I remember a game in the Hole in the Wall in Catlock, Montana: three players with four-of-a-kind natural. There was a pot to write home about, and me dropping out with a busted flush. I was lucky."

"For the tenth time, Perry, what in the world are we going to do with a rundown bar in a rundown town, a rundown—"

"T.G., T.G., for the tenth time, stop grousing and count your blessings. For the first time in your life you are the owner of real estate, a tangible piece of the county, a building, fixtures, a well-stocked bar, a bartender. Why must you deliberately blind yourself to the possibilities? The world's your oyster!"

"What possibilities? A rundown bar in a rundown—"

Perry cut him off with a theatrical flourish of his hand. "Please, let me go on. If you'd listened to what Mary Alice Tubbs said last night, you'd remember that this burg, Muddy Springs, sits smack dab on the Chisholm Trail. Making it a veritable gold mine that's never been opened. In a week the month of June will be upon us. Our timing couldn't be better. At this very moment herd upon herd of cattle are wandering north, heading straight for us."

"I know, I heard her, only the Chisholm Trail's not the only trail north. What about the Shawnee, the Western, the Goodnight-Loving, even Fletcher's Route?"

"We're talking upward of a million head annually. There has to be more than one route. The grass and water would never sustain such a horde along one route. The only real competition for central Kansas is the Western Trail, and everybody knows that breaks off westerly a couple hundred miles from Chisholm.".

"Fletcher's doesn't. It follows it straight through Indian territory and stays with it all the way up to Dodge City."

"Bother Dodge City. I'm talking Caldwell on up to Ellsworth on the west branch of the Chisholm; Wichita, Newton, and Abilene to the east." Perry had knelt at the edge of the sidewalk and was drawing in the dust with the butt of his stogie. "Muddy Springs is the first settlement over the border. Before Caldwell." He straightened and flung his butt away. "T.G., if we move fast, we'll have time to turn this dump into a paradise for the drovers. We can order gambling equipment by the freight carload; we can afford it. Keep the front room just the way it is, maybe get rid of the Filipino plank Cutshaw calls a bar and replace it with something twice as wide, and longer; there's room. And fill the back room with equipment. Hire a few beauties to steer the thirsty, weary, and unwary back to the chuck-a-luck cages, the roulette wheel, the faro and dice tables, the poker . . ."

"I don't know . . ."

"Great Caesar's ghost, if you're not the grandfather of all pessimists! You're being ridiculous, as shortsighted as a blindman. Open your head, unlock your mind, look at the possibilities!"

"Look at the headaches. Where will we get help, the roving raving beauties you mentioned? The few women I've seen in this town make Mary Alice look like Lillian Russell."

"We'll import them. It's done all the time. People flock to good wages, and we'll pay top. We'll hire a couple of musclebound types to keep order, I myself will supervise the cutting of the whiskey, we can renovate the place top to bottom in a week—a hosing down and a coat of cheap paint should do wonders. I'll wire Hunsecker's in Chicago and order the equipment. Emil Hunsecker is good for at least thirty percent off, seeing as we'll be ordering in quantity. And he's got everything. He's got a roulette wheel with a built-in tilter on a spring; no need for any kind of magnets."

"Hold everything. Wouldn't it be better to get honest equipment? Whatever we decide on, the odds will favor the house; they always do. We'll be in business a lot longer and stay a lot healthier if we don't deliberately cheat the customers."

"Don't be asinine. Drovers aren't customers; they're cattle driving sheep just begging to be sheared. That reminds me, we should order at least a hundred decks of marked cards from Will and Finck in San Francisco. They make the best in the business."

"No marked cards!"

"My boy—"

"No rigged equipment."

"Not even a dice edge-shaver? They're only two bucks and they'll pay for themselves in the first hour."

"No."

"Will and Finck has nail prickers, acid for shading cards, trimming plates, cutters, everything. And cheap."

"No."

"Not even a couple dozen pair of metal loaders for the bird cages? The magnet goes under the table directly under the cage."

"I know where it goes. So do half the drovers heading this way. No."

"Will and Finck has a dice cup that's the cleverest thing you've ever seen. There's a secret chamber in the bottom that can swallow up legitimate dice and release rigged ones into the game. It can even handle a set of five eight-sided poker dice."

"No."

"A few off-center gambling tops? Just a few?"

"No."

"Coward."

"Bloodsucker."

"Balderdash! I never realized how yellow your belly actually is. It's a shock and a disappointment, my boy. I rest my case."

"Bless you."

"What you're saying is if we play it straight, honest as the preacher, you'll go for it."

"I don't know." Horne flicked his butt hissing into the horse trough. "I don't know as I'd like to settle here. It's about as exciting as solitary confinement."

"You just wait till the drovers show. You want excitement? They'll bring it by the barrelful."

"That's what I'm afraid of."

"We'll have bouncers, we'll make them check their guns at the door . . ."

"Speaking of guns, remind me: first thing tomorrow I want to replace my forty-five, my twenty-two Sharps derringer, Barns boot pistol, and dagger-mounted knuckle-duster."

"Dagger-mounted knuckle-duster—you've carried one for ten years and never once used it."

"It's nice to know it's handy if I need it."

"You wouldn't dare use it. You might accidentally carve somebody up, and you know what the sight of blood does to your stomach juices. How can anybody so capable, so talented, be so softhearted and cowardly?"

"I wasn't cowardly back at the table, was I? How much did you win, Mr. Spleen?"

"Beside the point. Well, what'll it be? Are we or aren't we going into business? Legitimate business that could flourish, could make fortunes for both of us. Like picking gold up off the ground. And keep in mind, it doesn't have to be forever. We can milk the goat for two years, then cash in. We could probably sell the whole works for fifty thousand, maybe even a hundred."

Horne yawned and stretched. "I'm tired. Let's talk about it in the morning, okay? Please? It's a big step, I need a clear head."

"If you insist."

"Let's go back to the hotel and turn in."

They started out. Two blocks ahead a tall red-haired man emerged from the night, coming toward them. He seemed to be in a fog. He walked mechanically, his every movement robotlike. His eyes were fixed straight ahead of him. He passed without looking at them. Horne slowed and looked at him. He appeared utterly crushed as they drew closer to him, but by the time they passed, his defeated expression was displaced by one that could only be described as murderous intent.

"Sore loser, your friend Cutshaw," murmured Perry.

"Shhhh."

On they walked in silence. Cutshaw's steps faded behind them.

"One question," said Horne as they drew within sight of the hotel. "You were dealing; did you cull that straight flush out of the discards of the previous hand and stack the deck for me?"

"I most certainly did not!"

"You sure?"

"Don't be a ninny. I'd have had to stack his straight flush and the other three competing hands as well, wouldn't I?"

"Not necessarily."

"My boy, it was genuine; they all were. Two straight flushes in the same suit. And coming out of the chute, no

less, not a single card drawn. Remarkable. Amazing. It's
fate, T.G."

"What?"

"It's preordained. You won the Cockeyed Coyote because you were destined to. Destined to own it, run it,
make your fortune from it. Fate. You can't avoid it; don't
even try."

4

Two weeks later the gambling equipment arrived, was uncrated and installed in the back room of the Cock-eyed Coyote. While they waited for it, Horne and Perry had both rooms completely renovated, the maroon and yellow wallpaper steamed off, the game trophies taken down, the framed paintings—most of which were wretchedly, amateurishly executed—disposed of, and a new mahogany bar installed, set atop the old one at the suggestion of the carpenter.

Horne had a new deed of ownership drawn up by a local attorney, properly notarized, framed, and hung on the wall over the cash drawer. Together he and Perry went through the liquor inventory bottle by bottle, at Horne's insistence discarding the harsher and life-threatening brands in favor of properly distilled spirits; they added a few fine French brandies to the liquors and doubled the beer-keg order from the distributor in Wellington. Mary Alice Tubbs got double her money back and charitably contributed a bolt of green baize, which was cut into large pieces for the four poker tables. New lighting was installed in the back room and a small hole bored in the ceiling near the main light fixture, which would enable a hired watchdog to kneel among the rafters in the attic and peer down at the play, looking for professional and amateur cheating. In addition Horne planned to roam about the room playing mine host and also keeping his eyes peeled. Roy Pendleton would, as usual, keep his eye on the bar money and cash drawer, and Perry promised to keep his eye on Roy.

Albert Cutshaw had evidently left town; nobody had seen him for days. This came as something of a relief for Horne, but not Perry. He had sized up the former owner as a sore loser, and saw no reason to restrict the description to the poker table.

As one day followed another up to the arrival of the equipment from Hunsecker's Gambling and Entertainment Equipment, Devices and Necessities of Chicago, Horne waxed more and more sanguine over the new venture and their prospects for success. Word came the day the equipment arrived that the first herd had crossed the Washita River about 150 miles south down the Chisholm Trail, which, if all went well and according to schedule, would bring them into town in about two weeks.

This particular herd had started in southern Texas, coming from a spread near Victoria, where the natives sprinkled their southern accents with Spanish accents and the air smelled of salt from the Gulf of Mexico. At trail's end in Abilene they would have been in the saddle every day upward of ten weeks, having sweated through a destructively arduous, perilous, gut-wrenching, soul-racking experience guaranteed to turn smooth-faced youngsters into fully breveted cowboys.

For most of the journey they had followed the main north-trending old Chisholm Trail. The Chisholm was named after a Scotch-Cherokee trader, Jesse Chisholm, who had carved out part of the route as a straight, level wagon road, with easy river fords between south-central Kansas and his trading post on the Canadian River in Indian territory. It had opened as a cattle trail two years after the cessation of hostilities; in the next five years more than a million head had clomped and lowed and bawled up the road, which by then had been trampled in places to a width of two hundred to four hundred yards and had been cut by erosion below the level of the plains it traversed. Beside it lay the bones of cows killed in stampedes

and of calves shot at birth because they could not keep up
with the drives. There were as well the bones of humans,
interred in shallow graves—a drowned man pulled out
next to a river crossing, or an early-day trail herder or
settler cut down by Indians. Every man who set out knew
the risks and knew that en route he was considered less
valuable than the steers he drove. Yet he went eagerly,
testing himself against the unknown as other men had,
shouldering rifles and marching off to war or shipping out
before the mast. He did not think about the cattle barons
expending a mere penny or so per mile per head to get
their beef to market and reaping enormous profits. Did
not think about the brutal realities of life on the trail,
which could degrade a man to the point of forcing him to
lick horse sweat from a saddle when the chuck wagon ran
out of salt. Did not mind that, in return for two or three,
even four months of dust, thirst, blisters, deprivation,
heat, cold, and danger, he received a paltry hundred
dollars in hard wages, barely the price of a new hat and a
fancy pair of boots.

It had taken fifty days and four hundred miles just to
put Texas behind the first herd "northing." There had been
stampedes, dust storms, fighting among the men, rustlers,
and days that seemed like weeks on end without water. In
central Texas one morning, just north of Fort Worth, the
last settlement they'd encountered before arriving in Muddy
Springs, the sky opened, letting loose a cannonade of
hailstones the size of quail eggs, pelting birds and rabbits
to death, and raising welts on the men so bruising that
later the skin sloughed off. The storm had caused the
herd to drift off trail and scatter. The whole crew had
to ride in front of the drift and press the animals back
into line.

Good luck had been theirs crossing the Red River.
Arriving, they found it low enough to be waded. Easy
though it was to ford, man and beast, it represented
special hazards. For it was at the Red River that men and
cattle left the protection of the law of the state of Texas
and entered the Nations, Indian territory settled by Cher-

okees, Creeks, Seminoles, Choctaws, and Chickasaws, and crisscrossed by the fierce Kiowas and even fiercer Comanches. Here, at the primitive border village of Red River Station, squatting on the Texas bank at the easier ford, the trail boss weeded out the lazies and the bad actors in the crew and new hired hands. Easy though the ford was at the time of crossing, the river itself was underlaid with treacherous quicksand. The streamside trees captured tangles of driftwood in their higher branches, marking the high water of past floods. A scattering of rude graves near the station held the bodies of men killed attempting to cross.

Crossing Indian territory, the herd found lush grasses to feed on, and ample water. But for the drovers the work remained backbreaking. The men lived in their saddles, survived on black coffee, rubbed fiery tobacco juice in their eyes to stay awake, and somehow summoned the energy to keep the animals from stampeding whenever they smelled water ahead. And they could smell it ten miles distant.

On plodded man and beast, ignoring their exhaustion, lopping one grueling mile after another off the distance separating them from Muddy Springs.

Perry ambled about town cloaked in an air of impatience and with dollar signs gleaming in his bright blue eyes. He pestered the clerk at the Western Union office near distraction, asking for the latest word on the progress of the herd. The clerk insisted that he hadn't heard a thing, that trail bosses had no reason to wire their location to the towns in front of them. Rumors winged about like angry hornets. The Victoria herd had crossed the Red River, the Washita, and both Canadian branches, and was closing on the border. The Victoria herd had crossed the Red River and was bogged down on the south bank of the raging Washita. The Victoria herd had crossed King Fisher Creek, but at the next crossing, four days beyond, the river water had been found to be fouled from a huge deposit of alkali and the herd had to be deliberately stampeded across to prevent their drinking themselves to death. But once across the animals tried to double back, and the riders had to battle all night long and most of the next day to get them moving ahead again.

Old tales, mostly fictional, were attached to the drive by the more imaginative rumor-mongers among the towns-people.

"The Comanche are on the warpath again; already cut out half the herd and kilt at least a dozen drovers."

"They found six human skeletons with their shoes on north o' the Canadian. Kiowas, you betcha."

"They're bringing up the Texas fever. Jim Lawson's cousin wrote him a letter from Victoria. Said he saw them leave and half the herd were roach-backed, heads hanging low, ears drooping, eyes dull and glassy, and staggering. Texas fever, that's what they're bringing up. Can't sell sick cows in Abilene, that's for sure. Might just as well shoot what's left, turn around, and go home."

"They weren't two days out of Victoria before they discovered they had a couple stampeders in the bunch. Had to sew their eyelids shut. Thread took two weeks to rot; by that time the beeves were simmered down and easy as old cows to handle."

Horne paid little heed to rumors and speculation. He had too much to do supervising preparations. He had hired a second bartender to help Roy Pendleton during the anticipated rush. He'd also hired four scantily-clad lovelies to, as Roy put it, "pretty up the place." One of the girls—Star Hopwell, she called herself, setting Horne to wondering how well she did hop—sold herself as a faro and blackjack dealer. He tested her skills, not letting on that he was abundantly experienced at both games. She turned out to be good if not exceptional.

The finishing touch to the Cockeyed Coyote's overhauling was a fresh coat of varnish applied to the coyote itself. It gleamed resplendently above the entrance. Perry, at heart something of a snob, thought the head should come down and the saloon-cum-gambling casino be renamed something more dignified. He suggested the Drovers' Haven. Horne suggested his suggestion was dull; he liked the Cockeyed Coyote. It was undignified perhaps, but colorful, creative. He'd never heard the name before. Cockeyed Coyote it remained.

Late on a Tuesday afternoon in the last week in June a lone rider came dusting into town, shouting the news: the Victoria herd had crossed the border and was only a mile from town.

5

Horne and Perry were well-prepared to greet, befriend, and fleece the visiting drovers, but ill-prepared for the mood they arrived in. They naturally assumed they'd let loose; to what degree was not easy to predict. Still, these were men who had weathered ten weeks of harsh living conditions, deprived of the commonest amenities, of decent food, clean clothing, and bathwater; comfortable beds and the companionship of the opposite sex. Their lot had been no better than that of men in prison, perhaps not as good: prisoners, after all, do have a roof over their heads, beds, creature comforts, and even, to some extent, privacy. Drovers have the sky, the ground, the work, and little else.

Into town they thundered, aching to raise hell and double-damned if they'd let anyone stand in their way. One hundred seventy-three of them—twenty left behind to watch the herd—dusty, weary, bored, wild-eyed, rip-roaring rawhiders all, firing six-guns and whooping like Sioux on the warpath. The staid and proper citizens of Muddy Springs took one look and rushed for cover. Those with more gravel in their gizzards and those with exploitation on their minds, held their ground and wide-eyed the spectacle. Riders knocked down overhang supports, stove through wooden sidewalks, overturned horse troughs, shattered windows, and inflicted other minor damage from one end of Main Street to the other. Stray bullets slightly wounded six locals and sent most of the others still outside racing for cover not already appropriated by the staid and proper contingent.

The trail boss's letter of credit was drawn on a bank in Abilene, the herd's final destination, but despite not having been paid their one hundred dollars—more or less, depending on old obligations and loans or other debts incurred en route—every man seemed to have some money of his own, at least enough for a night on the town. Tomorrow would see them back on the trail, so tonight was their night to howl. Dirty and disheveled, bearded and bathless, they flocked to the Silver Spur Saloon, McCabe's Dance Hall, and the Cockeyed Coyote. The two bouncers Horne had hired to keep order paled visibly at sight of the raucous mob bearing down on the swinging doors, some of the men still firing their guns in the air and whooping loudly. Horne stood behind his bouncers with Perry behind him and Roy and the other bartender behind Perry, and the four buxom young ladies behind the bartenders, watching. Horne could feel his cheeks drain of color.

"They'll tear the place apart," rasped Perry behind him, reading his thoughts.

Horne stepped between the bouncers and held up his hands. "Slow down, boys. You're all welcome, but kindly enter two at a time only, okay? Two by two and give up your guns to the bartenders. They'll be tagged with your name, you'll be given a receipt, and you can pick them up on your way out. House rules, boys, enter two by two, surrender your—"

He did not get to finish. The oncoming horde paid not the slightest attention, bulling forward en masse, funneling through the doors, elbowing owner, uncle, and employees alike out of their path.

"Gentlemen, gentlemen," boomed Horne, staggering backward, gripping his stomach where an errant elbow had hammered it. "Gentlemen, two at a time, please. Please?"

In they poured, in the process knocking one of the batwing doors off its hinges and the other off its top hinge. Perry angrily wrenched it completely free and tossed it to one side. Not a single arrival laid his six-gun on the bar as Horne had requested, as the large sign with the six-inch

letters taped to the mirror ordered. Up to the bar they
bellied and in a twinkling were standing four deep, shouting drink orders, sweeping the girls into their midst and
persisting in paying no attention to Horne, positioned
behind them, pleading for attention.

Perry sidled up to him. "It's useless," he boomed. "You're
wasting your breath."

"What did you say? I didn't hear."

"Leave them alone. Don't pester them, you'll only turn
'em surly."

Roy and the other bartender raced back and forth behind the bar dispensing drinks, hurling money into the
cash drawer, some of it missing and landing on the floor. A
drink in one hand, a bottle in the other, one drover after
another drifted to the rear of the room. One pulled the
back door open.

"Hey, boys, looky here! Gamblin'!"

"Poker, bird cages, keno gooses, tigers . . ."

"Gallopin' dom'nos, vingt-et-un, roo-letty, evvythin'!"

As they'd surged through the front door, they over-
flowed into the casino. Horne, Perry, and the girls followed.

"There's nearly twenty-five hundred dollars' worth of
brand-new equipment," rasped Perry. "If any of them so
much as bends a bird cage, I'll take him apart."

"Sure you will," blared Horne over the persisting ear-
splitting clamor. "Great God, I hope I don't go deaf before
they go broke."

"What did you say?"

"Nothing, nothing."

A few of the more civilized intruders, very much the
minority, took chairs at the poker tables, where the house
supplied them with cards and chips at a price. Others set
upon the gambling devices. In seconds dice were clicking,
the roulette ball was rattling, and the slap of cards could
be heard through the babbling. The two bouncers, both
wearing six-guns, had mysteriously vanished. Much too
quickly, as Horne's pounding heart signaled, the drovers'
diversion began to show signs of getting out of hand. The
girl in charge of the roulette wheel was surrounded by a
dozen men. While the wheel was spinning, the ball click-

ing merrily in the opposite direction, one of the drovers
lifted the wheel, dropping the ball into number 14. The
others protested loudly, the girl tried to wrest the wheel
from his grasp, another man snatched up the ball, and
tossed it in his mouth like a pill. All hell broke loose. The
tilter grabbed the ball stealer by the shirtfront and knocked
him cold. One of the poker players jumped to his feet and
flipped the table over, scattering cards, chips, and money,
drawing a chorus of resentful bellowing from the others.
Horne stood rooted, casting about helplessly. One man
had seized a bird cage and was pulling the bars apart to
get at the dice.

"They're loaded! They're loaded!"

A fight erupted at one of the faro tables. One man drove
a haymaker into another's head, toppling him squarely
onto the table, caving it in. A gun went off, then two
more. In the door came a drover on horseback, drunk,
swaying in his saddle, yelling at the top of his lungs. His
arrival stopped the budding free-for-all for a split second,
then off his horse he fell, triggering a resumption of the
onslaught.

Fights were breaking out all over the room. Bottles,
keno gooses, a bird cage, and legs from the shattered faro
table were pressed into service as weapons. Horne espied
Perry edging toward the door to the bar, his eyes fear-
stricken. He shouldered between two combatants to follow him out. He was grabbed from behind and pulled
down. Suddenly confronted by a forest of legs, he struggled to rise before he got trampled; got to his knees, got to
his feet, and again set his course for the door and escape
from the bedlam.

To his left one of the girls was up on a drover's back,
riding him and swinging a chair leg at a man who tried to
pull her down, whacking him, felling him. The sounds of
fists, wood and metal against bone, the blasting of six-
guns, yelling, screaming, and shattering equipment bela-
bored Horne's eardrums. The light fixture depending from
the center of the ceiling was shot free of its mooring,
plummeting, striking a man full in the skull, knocking him
out. But hemmed in as he was, he could not fall. Instead,

he stood gaping sightlessly, his tongue lolling from his mouth, bits of glass dusting his shoulders.

Horne reached the door and, turning, took one last look at the melee, just as a drover smashed another against the wall two feet from him, caving it in. The riderless horse was swinging about in confusion, neighing loudly, shifting its head one way then the other, ignored by the combatants.

Horne turned to go. The bar was as mobbed as the casino. He espied Perry's snow-white mane at the far end of the bar and started for him, calling his name loudly. He took two steps and an anvil struck the back of his head, crimson flares leapt from his brain in a star burst and he crumpled.

His head felt as if a tree had fallen on it. It ached viciously, threatening to explode. His eyes felt as if twin branding irons were testing his sockets. He closed them and kept them closed. His brain felt like it had torn loose and was spinning inside his skull.

"You okay?" He recognized Perry's voice. "Open your eyes, T.G."

"No."

"T.G. . . ."

He opened them. The branding irons drilled deeper, touching his forebrain. Again he closed his eyes, but not before he got a glimpse of his surroundings. They were in the office of Marshal Ned Bronkowski. For a fleeting second Horne saw him sitting fat, wheezing and sweating in his screw-and-spring office chair at his curtain-top desk.

He could hear fighting: heavy breathing, scuffling, fists pounding, smashing bone. Two somebodies were fighting, and Perry sat beside him ignoring them. Bronkowski ignored them. His curiosity aroused, Horne grit his teeth and once more opened his eyes. Two drovers, their shirts ragged, knuckles raw, faces bruised and slashed, staggered about swinging wildly, making contact now and then, panting like winded horses, blood streaming from both their noses, both rapidly tiring. One hit the other, dropping him. To Horne's left were three cells in a line, all small, barely able to accommodate their five-foot wall cots, all crammed with prisoners. Sardines could not have been packed more tightly. Everyone was forced to stand.

"Darryl," barked the marshal. "Two more."

A deputy came forward, his key ring jangling from his belt. Seizing the unconcious man under the arms, he dragged him across the blood-spattered floor.

"Move it," snapped the marshal to the victor, without even looking at him.

The man obediently followed. The deputy got the loser up to the cell door, lifted him to his feet, held him upright against the bars with one hand, unlocked the door with the other, nodded the winner inside, and pushed the loser after him.

"Not here," bawled one of the occupants. "Ain't no room!"

"One o' the others," exclaimed another man. "We're so tight we cain't hardly breathe."

Their pleas were ignored, the door closed and relocked, the key ring restored to its nail over the marshal's desk by Darryl.

"They're right, Ned," he said, "we can't fit another mother's son in any one of the three cells."

"Who hit me?" asked Horne, sending his left hand up to the top of his head, touching a turkey-egg-sized lump tentatively and wincing. "Ooooo . . ."

"Are you going to do something, Marshal, or not?" Perry asked. "They're tearing the place apart."

"What do you expect me to do? I got four deputies, three of 'em out collaring the worst offenders. Trying their damnedest to stabilize the sitution, which is next to impossible. They're only outnumbered fifty to one. The more we round up, the more go berserk. They're tearing up the whole goddamned town. What the hell do I care about the Coyote?"

"Tearing up the town while you sit on your duff whining."

"Why did whoever hit me hit me?"

"What do you expect me to do? Run over there and make a goddamned speech? I warned you the day you came to me and told me you wanted to open a goddamned gambling hall, you'd better be prepared for hell on wheels when the herders hit town. The Coyote, the Silver Spur, and the dance hall are fair game for the worst they can do. I warned you."

"I never even saw it coming."

"Our place of business has as much right to the protection of the law as the next place. More, since as you say we're one of their prime targets."

"So why didn't you go into the undertaking business? Goddamned gambling joint is like waving a red flag in front of a bull. I warned you, I did."

"Anybody see who hit me?"

The door flew open. In stomped a giant deputy with one eye blackened and so puffed it was reduced to a slit. In each hand he held a drover by the collar, both unconscious and limp as rags.

"Two more, Ned."

"There's no room left," bawled Darryl.

"Full up, Everett," said the marshall, "take 'em . . . take 'em over to the stable. Tell Jake Farnsworth we're full, it's an emergency, we need the corral out back. Tell him it's just for the night. Whatever horses he's got in there he can stable for the time being. You go along, Darryl. Take a rifle. Everett, stick them in the pen and any others you collar. Lock them in. Darryl, you'll stand guard. Everett, you relieve him in four hours. Get along, both of you."

The man in Everett's left hand groaned.

"I think my skull's fractured," murmured Horne.

Perry bristled. "Oh, shut up, T.G., we've got troubles enough without your whining."

Darryl and Everett trooped out with the prisoners.

"I did warn you," repeated Bronkowski to Perry. In a tone that had a bit of a guilty ring to it, noted Horne.

"A fine kettle of fish," boomed Perry. "A fine way to treat two respectable businessmen."

"Oh, shut up. If you're so damned worried about your property, what the hell are you doing here pestering me? Why aren't you back at the Coyote grabbing the worst of the lot?"

"Give us a deputy and we'll do just that," asserted Perry.

"Deputies are all tied up. What are you, blind? You've got bouncers, put them to work."

"They lit out."

Bronkowski snorted, slapped his knee, and cackled derisively. "Chrissakes, they're the only ones with any sense. For the last time, we can't help you any more than we already are; we're doing the best we can. It's starting to get dark out. Another half-hour or so things should begin to quiet down. We'll have the worst of the lot behind bars or in the corral, and the rest'll be so drunk they won't be able to move."

"Another half-hour and the Coyote will be leveled," boomed Perry.

"Good! Good riddance to bad rubbish. Why don't you get smart? Why don't you go out and find the trail boss? Give him an earful; find out who owns the herd down in south Texas, get his name; he's responsible for the conduct of his employees."

"Balderdash! You're talking through your hat and you know it. You ought to be ashamed to wear that badge. You're a disgrace to it. Damned if I don't report you to the state's attorney general!"

Bronkowski's round, aging cherub's face hardened. He rose from his chair.

Horne groaned. "I know it's fractured. I can tell. I have to see a doctor."

"Mendenhall, Marblehall, whatever you call yourself, you get on your feet and get the hell out of here, and take your friend Mr. Flasharity with you. Beat it and don't come back. Ever!"

Horne stood outside with Perry. Perry lit a stogie. Shooting echoed up and down the street. A woman screamed and laughed hysterically. What sounded like a barrel dropping from a roof caught Perry's attention, coming from the alley to their left. Horne filled his lungs. Deprived of the sun's heat, the air was cool and sweet to the taste. His knees felt wobbly and nausea flooded his stomach. His head felt like two halves of a melon, cleanly split, revealing the pulp and seeds.

"Did you see who hit me?"

"No, and will you quit asking? Who cares? I don't. Let's go back to the Coyote."

"Must we? I want to see a doctor."

"Later. I want to see the extent of the damage. We really shouldn't have deserted Roy and the new man, or the girls. Damn Bronkowski!"

"He's got his hands full."

"And his fat duff glued to his chair."

Horne weaved and stumbled once, then again, as he followed Perry down the sidewalk. At the corner they crossed the street. Groups of drovers wandered about yelling, shooting, waving bottles and drinking from them. One carried a naked mannequin pilfered from La Paree Millinery Shop, its front window shattered across the way. They passed a horse trough with two men passed out in it, fast asleep, with beatific smiles wreathing their bristle-studded faces. Diagonally across the way, the Cockeyed Coyote stared down from its perch. Yellow light poured out the doorless entrance.

They drew closer. Something was wrong; Horne instinctively felt it before he realized what it was. All was quiet inside. They crossed the street and approached. The door to the rear room was closed. The bar was empty. Tables and chairs were overturned, smashed bottles and glasses littered the floor. The new mahogany bar had been wrenched loose, revealing the old one in place. The mirror behind it was shattered in a dozen places. The room looked as if a tornado had blown in, bent, broke, and smashed everything in its path, and departed.

"Oh, my God," murmured Horne.

Perry frowned worriedly. "Where is everybody?"

"Dead. Murdered. Let's not go in."

"We've got to. I want to see the casino."

"You go, I'll wait here for you."

Perry sputtered and exploded, grabbing him by the sleeve, pushing him roughly ahead. In they went.

6

Horne consciously tried to steel himself for the sight that would meet his aching eyes when they opened the door. But open it they could not. It moved about an inch clear of the jamb and no farther. Together they shouldered it wide enough for one, then the other to slip inside. They found Horne's new hat wedged under the door, fallen from his head when he had fallen. He snatched it up and flung it angrily across the room. The door to the backyard stood ajar. Horne took one look and leaned against the door where he had watched one of the drovers slam another through the wall shortly before his own lights went out.

The place was a perfect shambles. The roulette wheel was broken into small pieces, the bird cages looked stomped on, cards and chips were scattered about, and every stick of furniture smashed. The glass light fixture that had been shot loose and fallen on the man lay in a thousand pieces; all the other lights and every wall decoration were ruined. Even the green baize that had draped the poker tables was ripped. Blood spattered the walls and floor.

Perry found a glass eye, two different colored plumes, part of two of the girls' hairdos, a broken croupier stick, a faro board with hoof prints, a brassiere, a half-filled bottle of Warner's Safe Kidney Cure, and a wallet with thirty pesos in it.

There were bullet holes everywhere, with the ceiling

the primary target, and more broken glass was scattered about there than out front.

Horne hung his head, closed his eyes, braced his brain against the persisting throbbing, and felt a part of himself die. A lonesome night freight chugged through his soul, its whistle hooting mournfully. And the pain trapped in his skull intensified.

"It looks like the Second Battle of Bull Run," rasped Perry. "Not a stick can be salvaged. Two hundred and fifty dollars for that ceiling lamp alone. Look at the chuck-a-luck cages. Look T.G."

"Let's get out of here. My head is getting worse. It's possible I'm dying. Can you die standing? When you're hit on the head, does your brain swell? Mine feels like it. I need a doctor, really."

"Later."

"Now, dammit! Ooooo." He scowled and stalked out of the place.

"Wait, wait . . ."

Perry came up beside him out front. "Did you notice, somebody grabbed your deed off the wall. It's not there, it's not on the floor."

"They're welcome to it. Where's the nearest doctor?"

"There's a sign around the corner two or three doors down. I don't recall the name."

"Who cares? As long as he's the real thing and can check me out, give me a pill or something for the pain. At this point I'd even pay him to put me out of my misery."

Off he swept, striding to the corner, rounding it, pulling up short, gaping and gasping. A line of waiting patients stretched from the doctor's office door up the slate sidewalk, through the little gate and down the dirt walk at least ten yards. It looked like a troop of walking wounded survivors from a full-scale battle. Many wore makeshift bandages around their bleeding heads; others displayed half-covered faces; there were men with broken arms in slings. A couple, unable to find cloth, supported their forearms with rope. Other men were supported by friends, helping them take their weight off broken legs. Some were missing teeth, spitting blood, nursing broken noses or black eyes, or pressing bloodstained rags against facial cuts. One man seemed to be holding his left ear to his head. Another was throwing up over the little picket fence into the doctor's nasturtiums. It was human suffering on parade. They groused, grimaced, grumbled, griped, and groaned. Not one gave Horne or Perry so much as a glance.

"This is impossible," Horne burst. "I'll be six hours in line. I'll be dead by the time I move up to the gate. Let's go." He started back the way they had come.

"Where?"

"The stables. We'll ride out to Mary Alice's; she'll take care of me. Better somebody I know than a sawbones I've never laid eyes on, anyway."

Jake Farnsworth's stable was on the brink of collapse. Horne fleetingly wondered why the drovers hadn't noticed and pushed it flat. They found Farnsworth out back keeping Darryl company while the deputy guarded the pen partially filled with prisoners. They sat on the ground, leaning against the fence, swapping bottles and chatting amiably. As peaceful, noted Perry, as a Quaker choir. Darryl greeted them. Jake got out their horses and helped saddle them.

"Some goins-on," he commented. "Ain't been hell raised this much in Muddy Springs since Hector was a pup. Drovers comin' up the Chisholm Trail usually just pass on through. Must be the Cockeyed Coyote startin' up gamblin' was the big 'traction made 'em stop off this time. How'd you boys do?"

"Splendidly," grumbled Perry.

Horne grunted and mounted his big bay. Off they rode in the direction of the Tubbs farm.

"You and your harebrained get-rich-quick schemes," Horne muttered. "Why I listen to you, why I never learn, beats me. Four thousand dollars down the drain, not to mention all that work, the preparation, the investment in the equipment, hiring people. My ears are beginning to ring; this is permanent, I know it is. It's getting worse and worse. I'll end up in a wheelchair babbling, dribbling out of the corner of my mouth, unable to control my bladder, feed myself. Brain damage does that to you, you know."

"Oh, stop whining!"

"Why did I let you talk me into it?"

"I didn't. It was your greedy little voice. And it wasn't get-rich-quick, it was a sound businesss investment. Can I help it if we were invaded by the Mongol horde?"

"Oh, come on, you knew all along they'd be this bad, this destructive, wild—"

"You didn't?"

"I don't want to talk about it. Talking hurts my head. Riding does, breathing, just thinking . . . How far to Mary Alice's?"

"Another four miles. I'm sorry about your head, T.G., but I'm sure it's not fractured."

"Mmmmmmm."

They rode on in silence rendered icy by Horne's scowl. The air had mysteriously warmed and become sultry since the two of them had come out of the marshal's office. Perry had retrieved Horne's hat when he flung it across the room, had reshaped it for him as best he could, and Horne had put it on. His aching head felt as if it was filling the hat with heat, radiating it upward to the crown, then settling back down to drape the top of his head. He removed his hat and tucked it under his arm. If he could make it through the night, he thought, he just might survive. Mary Alice would confirm his skull was fractured. It had to be. He'd been hit in the head countless times, knocked out dozens, and never but never felt pain like this.

The house showed the same lonely light in the front window they had seen getting off the train more than three weeks earlier. By the time they hobbled the horses and started toward the front door, Horne's legs were so rubbery, so weak was he, Perry had to hold him upright.

Mary Alice greeted his knock effusively. "My stars, look who's here." Her face darkened and assumed a pitying expression as she noticed Horne's condition. "My gracious, Al, come in, come in."

*   *   *

"It's only a concussion."

"You can't be sure."

"It's not fractured, I tell you. You don't have blood or anything else coming out your mouth or ears or nose. No double vision. Your pupils are identical, not uneven in size, not contracted to pinpoints or unusually dilated. You're not drowsy, no convulsions, blacking out. You can still speak clearly. Concussion, son. I'm sorry to be the bearer of such disappointing news."

Perry laughed. Horne riveted him with a scowl calculated to kill a healthy plant. Mary Alice had bandaged his head and put him to bed. Lying down helped ease his discomfort. He no longer felt nauseous. Perry detailed the goings-on in town and the unhappy fate of the Cock-eyed Coyote.

"I wish I could say I'm surprised," rejoined Mary Alice when he had finished, "but knowing drovers . . ."

"One definite thing has come out of this nightmare," said Horne "The Coyote certainly hasn't endeared itself to Muddy Springs. People are going to point at us and accuse us of lighting the fire. We provided the big attraction . . ."

"I disagree," said Perry. "There's always an element that looks down its noses at gambling and boozing, and they'll always say I told you so, but we're not responsible for the carrying on all over town. Two-thirds of the drovers never came near the Coyote, and still got into trouble."

"You should have hired bouncers," said Mary Alice.

"We did," said Perry. "They lit out. They're probably halfway to Kansas City by now, the lily-livered degenerates. Rascals!"

Mary Alice frowned. "I don't want to criticize, Ben, but the way you tell it, it sounds like you didn't take all the precautions you should have. You could have stopped them outside the front door, made them check their guns before they even set foot inside. A gun gives a drunk one heck of a lot of gumption. Without a gun, drunk or sober, you can make him toe the line a lot easier. And you could have restricted the number you let in at one time. Keep it down to thirty or forty, manageable size."

"That's all water over the dam now," said Horne.

"They'll be moving out tomorrow. You'll have time to clean the place up, fix things up before the next drive comes to town."

"We have no intention of fixing the place up," Horne said testily. "This was my first and last business venture. It turned out a debacle. I've learned my lesson, thank you. When I get back on my feet, I'll clean the place up, pay off the help, and sell out to the highest bidder. Sell at a loss if I have to. Anybody can have it, lock, stock, and barrel, for a thousand even."

He did a double-take at Perry, staring at him.

"I've always known you to be somewhat irresolute at times," Perry said quietly, "but I never thought of you as a quitter."

"Discretion's the better part of valor, my friend."

Perry snickered. "As Cervantes so aptly put it: the brave man carves out his fortune."

"You carve, I'll watch. On second thought, I won't be around. As soon as I'm fit to travel, that's exactly what I'm going to do."

"Pay no attention to him, Mary Alice, he's upset. Clear thinking will prevail when he's back on his feet."

"Let me ask you a silly question, Al. Hypothetical question. If you hadn't converted the back room into a casino, if all you had to offer was just the bar out front, do you think they would have wrecked it?"

"You're right," said Horne. "It is a silly question."

"Maybe bringing in all that gambling equipment was a mistake; maybe you should have stuck to poker. Poker players get mad, blow up, but usually only one at a time and they can be handled. The other players'd do the handling for you. Dice and faro and chuck-a-luck and roulette, ten, fifteen people can get mad, stir up everybody else, raise the roof."

"Good point," Perry said.

"It's a little late to consider possible variations," said Horne. "I mean it, Perry, I'm through playing mine host, through entrepreneuring. Keeping a horde of ignoble savages in line is beyond my capabilities. Marshall Bronkowski and his four deputies couldn't have controlled that mob.

Now that I think about it, the two of us were lucky to get out alive. I hope none of the girls was injured."

He was suddenly feeling drowsy. He fisted a yawn.

"Hungry?" asked Mary Alice. "I've got vegetable soup on the stove, or would you rather nap?"

"Nap . . ."

They left him in privacy. She invited Perry into the kitchen to sample her soup.

"That was a short fling in business," she said.

"Pay no attention, he's just shooting off his mouth. It's simple. All we do is restore the place and beef up our security. Hire half a dozen bouncers; and I like your idea to make them check their weapons outside before we even let them through the door. I mean, if Abilene and Dodge City can accommodate a bunch of drovers, entertain them, let them raise hell and spend their cash, why can't Muddy Springs? Hays City, Ellsworth, Newton, Wichita, they've all made money off cattle drives. And they don't worry about the bluenoses; gambling's what's made this country great, and a cattle town without it is a sure loser. Ever hear of Edward Chase?"

"How's the soup?"

"Delicious. Edward Chase owns the Progressive in Denver. A giant in the field. He keeps the roulette wheels spinning in just about every casino in town. He provides a service that's needed; he does it well, he's done it for fifteen years and he's worth a fortune."

"Probably because he doesn't have to cater to drovers, not in Denver."

"Drovers are people, Mary Alice. They may be more high-strung than miners and ordinary folks, because of what they're put through. Thirstier, hungrier for a good time after so many weeks of slave labor, but they're human. They just need closer supervision."

"That's putting it mildly."

"He's not going to throw in the sponge. Not this soon, not after all we've gone through. It'd be like tearing up money and throwing it in the gutter. The Cockeyed Coyote is a gold mine, it can't help but be. It could become bigger, more prominent and popular than the Bird Cage in Tomb-

stone. Could be a magnet for every herd coming north.
Gambling is a mania in the West; everybody, even the
Indians, gambles. The Cockeyed Coyote is the goose that
laid the golden egg."

"Aren't you mixing similes or metaphors or something?"

"I'm serious."

"I should say you are, but I'm not the one you have to
convince."

"I know, I know. Don't worry, I'll talk him into it. You
know, maybe the best stragegy would be to ease him
back into it. Take your idea of turning the casino into a
poker parlor, not replace the equipment, keep it strictly
cards. Of course, poker's the slowest way of making money.
Roulette, faro, almost everything else is ten times as fast."

"You like money, don't you, Ben?"

"I . . . Does it show that bad?"

"You should see your eyes and the way you lick your
lips. Tell me something. If you made a million, what
would you do with it?"

"Turn it into ten. There's no limit to how much I could
run it into."

"If you ran it into a hundred million, what would you
do with that? What I'm getting at, is what in the world
can you do with a million dollars? Make yourself healthier?
Happier? More respected? A better person? Can you buy
a place in heaven? Will your wife or girlfriend or children
love you any more if you're rich? Mind you, I don't know,
I'm just asking."

"Can I please have a little more soup? It really is
delicious."

By the next afternoon Horne was sufficiently recovered
to get out of bed and ride back to town. Perry discreetly
avoided any suggestion, even a veiled hint that they go
back into business. Muddy Springs looked like a ghost
town when they got there. There was no shortage of
damage up and down Main Street, but no sign of the
drovers, who, in keeping with their schedule, had pulled
out early that morning. Horne wondered if their numbers
included most or all of the walking wounded. They must

have included Marshal Bronkowski's arrests. Happy to be rid of them, he'd no doubt let them go without even fining them. They rode up to the Cockeyed Coyote, dismounted, and hitched to the rail.

"You see what I see?" Perry asked.

The swinging doors had been restored. They pushed inside. The bar had been cleaned up. Roy was alone behind the bar, busy polishing glasses. The ranks of bottles lining the shelves behind him, duplicated in the heavily damaged mirror, were noticeably thinned. He greeted them, taking note of Horne's bandaged head.

"You okay, Boss?"

"He's fine," said Perry. "Where's your sidekick?"

"He quit. His wife made him. He brought home some shiner. The girls are still here, though. They're inside pickin' up."

"Your loyalty's most commendable, Roy. Isn't it, T.G.?"

"Mmmmm."

Star Hopwell and the other three girls had all but finished cleaning up. They greeted Horne and Perry pleasantly, expressing concern over Horne's head—especially Star. The look in her eye since Horne had first met her did not go unnoticed by him. But with all he'd had to do, and all that went on, he just hadn't gotten around to meeting her on anything other than an employer-employee basis.

Perry cleared his throat dramatically. "Ladies, I must say your loyalty is most commendable. Most. Isn't it, T.G.?

"Yes, yes . . ."

"We piled everything out back," said a conspicuously well-endowed redhead, sporting a mole the size of a penny on her chubby left cheek. "None of the equipment was worth saving; it's all junk."

"We won't be needing it from now on anyway," said Perry. "We've decided to convert the casino into a poker room exclusively."

"Perry . . ."

"With the equipment out of the way, there should be room for at least four additional tables."

"Perry . . ."

"I know you know poker, Miss Hopwell. Do you other ladies? If you don't, don't be ashamed to admit it."

"Perry . . ."

"It's actually a fairly simple game. I'd be happy to sit down and teach you."

"I don't think that'll be necessary," Horne interposed.

"We only have a few more days before the next drive gets here," continued Perry. "If any of you want poker lessons, just raise your hands."

All four did.

"We'll start as soon as we can get some tables and chairs in here. Miss Hopwell, would you mind seeing to that? There must be some more available in the general store. Tell the clerk to charge them to our account. He knows us, we've done business before. We'll start with four tables, each one with seven round-back chairs. Not too expensive now. And make sure you ask for twenty percent off; we're entitled to a bulk discount."

"Perry . . ."

"And don't you carry anything back. Tell them you want everything delivered. As soon as possible."

They filed out.

"I do like your brass, Perry; like the way you squander my money without even bothering to ask."

"Why ask? You'd only put the kibosh on it. But you didn't, did you?" He clapped him on the back in friendly fashion. "It's a relief to see you've come to your senses. We'll resume with poker exclusively. If it turns out too slow to turn a decent dollar, we'll cross that bridge when we come to it. Perhaps add a single faro setup and a roulette wheel. One thing you have to admit, my boy, Roy and the girls are as loyal as they come—faithful to the cause. We didn't ask them to come back and clean up. They did it on their own. That's the sort of initiative one can't help but admire. And treasure. I do, don't you? They're a deserving bunch, bless them; imagine how they'd feel if we didn't pick up the pieces and start over. If we sneaked out of town with our tails between our legs, leaving them high and dry and unemployed."

"Oh, shut up!"

"I beg your pardon."

"Please listen. Just listen, don't talk. I gave it a try, my best shot."

"That you did."

"Tut. It turned out a disaster. No fault of ours, of anybody's other than the rabble responsible. I stood in this room last night and watched a pack of two-legged hyenas go totally berserk. It was frightening, Perry; for a time there I didn't think I'd make it to the door alive. I barely did. I don't know how Phil Coe does it in the Bull's Head Saloon up in Abilene. How Doc Thayer and Bill Pierce keep control in the Gold Rooms in Newton. They even offer Spanish monte; that's like holding a gun to somebody's head and demanding they fork over. I don't know how they do it and I don't care. Let's just say all three are better men than I am.

"Perry, I want out. Not tomorrow, not next week, now. I went to war, I fought, I survived, but fate may not be on my side a second time. I refuse to run a business that endangers my life. High-stakes poker with strangers is about as dangerous as I'm willing to try. Not this. Never again!"

"Do you think there's room for as many as eight tables? Each of us can move from table to table cleaning clocks, and clean up. When one guy goes broke, another takes his chair and you or I take him. Beautiful!"

"You're not listening."

"I heard every word you said. Only, you know what you did?" He leered demonically. "You tipped your hand."

"What are you talking about?"

"You held it all in until the girls were out the door. In the face of their loyalty and Roy's, you didn't have the nerve to tell them you were throwing in the sponge. I asked them to go shopping and you let them. Face it, T.G., only your mouth wants to quit. Your heart isn't in it."

"You're wrong. You can twist it sixteen different ways from breakfast with that devious, convoluted mind of yours, but you don't stand a chance. My mind is made up. When they start delivering the furniture I'll be standing at the front door. Horatius at the bridge: turning them back, telling them it's all a mistake, we're closing permanently.

"The Cockeyed Coyote goes on sale first thing in the morning. Price negotiable; very negotiable, incredibly! Put that in your pipe and smoke it."

"On second thought, why not start with six tables. We'll discuss it with the ladies when they get back. They're the best judges, since they're the ones who'll be walking around in here."

7

Perry stopped treating the situation so lightheartedly and got down to serious pleading, even wheedling. He trotted out every argument in favor of resuming business.

"It's no use, Perry. My mind is set in cement."

"I'm not surprised; stone and cement do complement each other well."

It remained for Star Hopwell to storm the bastion of Horne's obstinacy and overcome it. The girls came back about twenty minutes later. Star took Horne by the arm and moved him back outside, out of the others' hearing.

"T.G. Ah just want to say how grateful me and the othah girls are that you've decided to pick up wheah youh left off. Last night was rough as a cob; I saw that fella cream you with the bottle. It sure-nough takes a lotta backbone to shrug it off like youh doin', fohget 'bout it and go fohwahd.

"I worked in just about every dive in Nevada befoh I come back heah to Kansas. I stahted heah when Ah left Gawgia foh good back when. Workin' in Nevada Ah saw all kinds o' bosses. Most of 'em wasn't fit to run with the dogs. They use youh, 'buse youh, and toss youh aside like old shoes. They're skinflints, they cheat youh, and all most of 'em want is to getcha in bed."

On she talked. His eyes fell to her lovely breastworks, the planes gleaming with tiny beads of sweat, her breasts rising and falling as she breathed. It was the sort of sight that lent his cock a mind of its own. It twitched ever so

56

slightly and he imagined he could hear it moan. She smelled delectable—some floral scent. The sight of her eyes, huge and luminous, shining by their own light glowing from behind their irises, hurried his heartbeat. Her lips were unconsciously seductive as she formed her words and her voice was low, sensuous.

"Ah purely admire a man with a backbone. It's so rare. Most bosses Ah've seen would give up the ghost if they went through what we did heah last night. Most ain't got the guts of a yahdbird. Not you, you're all man, and us fouh count ouhselves lucky youh hihed us. You'll sure-nough get youh money's wuth. Youh got ouh respect and loyalty and we'll stick by till the last gun is fiahed, youh bet. Maybe that's the wrong way to put it; oh, hell, youh know what I'm tryin' to say. We're with youh, Roy too."

"I appreciate it, appreciate your telling me, Star."

"It's sure-nough from the haht. How's youh haid?"

"Lots better, thanks."

"The tables and chaihs'll be heah in a jiffy. Don't youh worry youh haid 'bout 'em, 'bout any piddlin' l'il details. We'll see to placin' them. If youh don't like how we set up, just say the wuhd and we'll change it 'round. Welcome home, T.G."

With this she impulsively bussed him on the cheek, smiled, laughed lightly, and went back inside.

Perry came out. He looked angry, but Horne attributed it more to disappointment.

"I'm going back to the hotel and pack. If you're selling, I see no reason to hang around. Roy can handle the transaction. As long as we leave him a forwarding address."

"Never mind."

"Never mind what?"

"We're not selling. We're . . . we'll . . . we'll give poker a try, dammit!"

"What are you so upset about?"

"Don't needle me, Perry, I'm not in the mood."

"Perish the thought. Is it permissible to ask what in the world changed your mind?"

"It is not. Forget it, I'm hungry, let's go eat."

*   *   *

The next three days were devoted to sprucing up the place: repairing the damaged wall, replacing the mirror, putting up three sections instead of one. Perry reasoned that it would be cheaper to replace a single, even two damaged sections than one entire piece. The old bar underneath the new one was removed, the new one set in its place. Another copy of the deed was obtained from Horne's attorney and hung in a frame in the spot vacated by its predecessor.

A huge liquor order was dispatched to the distributor in Wellington. It arrived the next day, was unpacked, and the bottles set on the shelves. Perry splurged, ordering a piano for the outside bar, which required two weeks to deliver, coming all the way from Kansas City. Horne advanced the girls money to buy new dresses. Roy hired a new bartender and six bouncers from among his friends in town. Perry made sure that they owned guns and knew how to use them.

He also measured both the front and rear entrances and sent off an order to Pittsburgh for two steel doors. During normal business hours they would be swung inward and locked against the wall. When the drovers arrived and descended on the Coyote, the doors would be swung into place, effectively blocking entry and exit. Horne and Perry would hold the only keys.

Shattered light fixtures were replaced; new green baize was measured and cut to fit the six new poker tables.

All was in readiness.

Horne walked Star home after the Coyote closed the night preparations were completed. She lived in a rooming house four doors down from the doctor's office. Walking by the office, he briefly wondered if all the patients had been taken care of. There was still blood on the slates leading from the gate to the front stoop.

On his best and most gentlemanly behavior, he bid Star good night at her door. Either she didn't hear him or didn't want to.

"Go 'round back and climb up the fiah staihs. I'll unlock the doah from the inside."

"What do you have in mind?"

"Same thing youh got, whatta youh think?"

She laughed and kissed him lightly on the cheek. He watched her go in and close the door. Then it opened again, her arm emerged, her index finger beckoned, and the door closed. He made his way down the side of the house to the rear and the stairs, nearly toppling a trash can en route. He was still not fully recovered from his braining of three nights before; his turkey egg remained full size, he entertained a slight headache, and he could tug his eyes and actuate pain. But nothing was wrong with his equipment.

He was halfway up the stairs when out of the pitch blackness above came the telltale sound of the door being unlocked and eased open.

"Coming, love, you bewitching minx you." He laughed lightly, the voice of the confident would-be conqueror. He reached the landing. The door stood wide, framing the ugliest woman he'd seen in ages. At first glance his stomach nearly turned over and his initial impression was that a caboose had been backed against her face, flattening every feature, including her lips, which sat her mouth like the rubber from a half-gallon mason jar. She leered lasciviously, pursing her rubber lips and sucked in noisily.

"Loverrrrr?"

"Oh, Lor' . . . I mean, my mistake. I thought you were somebody else."

"You're handsome."

"Thank you." He tried to wedge by her, but she effectively blocked the way, her massive frame all but completely filling the doorway.

"What's the rush?"

"It's my mother. I thought you were my sister. Mother's in her room waiting for me. She's sick as a dog, I have to take her to the doctor. I think it's her brain tumor acting up again."

Sympathy flooded the flattened visage. "Oh, can I help?"

"I appreciate the offer, but no. I'll manage. I'm in a bit of a hurry, the doctor's keeping the office open after hours for us."

She stood aside, let him pass, and started down the stairs. She sounded like an elephant descending a gangplank. He closed the door behind him and leaned against it to catch his breath. Star came around the corner carrying a lamp. She had changed into a kimono.

She took him by the hand and led him to her room. It was tiny, barely large enough to accommodate the bed, a single nightstand, washbasin, and chest of drawers. There was no chair, no closet, no armoire. So low was the ceiling, he instinctively lowered his head.

"Youh can stand straight, it's not that low."

"You're lucky you're a midget."

She had set the lamp down on the nightstand. The bed was turned down. She undid her sash, opened the flaps of her kimono, removed it, and stood in the circular swirl of it.

"Midget?"

Her breasts were enormous. One would have been more than enough. They looked somewhere between cantaloupes and small watermelons. But they didn't sag, riding high and proud, the baby-pink nipples studding them staring at him like widely separated eyes.

"Midget?" she repeated, snickering.

"My apologies. I never dreamed . . . With your blouse on . . . Why don't I just shut up?"

"Come heah, T.G."

He approached in the manner of a faithful dog responding to its master. What a body! What a wonderwork of nature! The curves, the angles, the hidden recesses, the overall voluptuousness. Sight of her had dried his mouth almost instantaneously; now he could feel sweat burst from his brow. He could feel his fingers opening and closing, the bones and joints beginning to ache in anticipation. Could feel his cock rising, forming an all-too-obvious bulge. Her limpid eyes slowly descended to it. She smiled.

"What's that?" Horne laughed nervously. "Let's see, shall we?"

By the time she got his clothes off—it took her all of forty seconds—his erection resembled the flagpole angling upward from the front of every statehouse in the nation. Sans flag, to be sure, but fully as hard as the staff.

"Oooooo, nice and hahd, and with its own l'il haht, poundin' and poundin'."

Down on her knees she went and slowly took his cock into her hot, moist mouth, driving the head down her throat and cleverly flexing her esophagus, massaging it, resting her rapidly swelling tongue for the flaying that was to follow. Her lips ringed the base of his cock. She began sucking and whipping. In spite of himself, gritting his teeth, straining, tensing his neck so hard his head quivered, he ejaculated almost at once. She pulled free, letting it splash all over her face and neck. Then, smiling up at him, sent forth her tongue to lick a circle around her mouth.

She washed her face, pulled him onto the bed, and went back to work on his cock. It reerected within seconds, becoming stiff as a poker. He mounted her and slowly penetrated. She came wildly alive, bouncing like a trampoline, her massive breasts slaping each other, pounding brutally, beating with a loud thwacking sound. He wondered why her cleavage wasn't a mass of bruises, but if it caused her any discomfort, it failed to show on her face. She pulled his head down and shoved her tongue halfway down his throat, soul-kissing him into near suffocation. They came together, his load flooding her quim, her load flooding his flooding. She squealed joyfully, continuing to buck like a mustang with a burr under its saddle.

They made the beast with two backs for the next hour with scarce a pause for rest between bouts, fucking until they were so spent they could barely move. They lay side by side studying the ceiling.

"That was fun," she whispered. "You're very good."

"You're marvelous, fantastic!"

"'Ah try. Ah like youh thingy."

"Me, too."

"Silly. Sereyusly, it's real thick; it touches me all ovah, it's special. Most are skinny or stumpy, youh's is man-sized: thick, wide. How'd it get so wide?"

"You really want to know?"

She raised up on one elbow and stared at him with a serious expression. "How?"

"When I was a tad, before I was old enough to use it, on winter days sitting in school I used to fold it under and sit on it to keep it warm. I guess over the years it just sort of flattened out."

She pushed his shoulder playfully. "Silly!"

"Cross my heart . . ."

She kissed him passionately. He felt like he was melting.

"Wanna make love?"

"I thought we were—"

"Some more, Ah mean."

"Can we let my thingy catch its breath a bit?"

"Just abit. Ah'm stahtin' to get real tingly down b'low. . ."

She lay back down. Neither spoke for a while. She broke the silence.

"Wha'cha thinkin' 'bout, T.G.?"

"Day after tomorrow when the thundering herd descends on us."

"Youh not worried, are youh?"

"Of course I'm worried. We could easily have a replay of the same debacle, maybe worse. Somebody could get killed."

"Not playin' pokah. It'll be all right, youh'll see. Youh got six bouncers, real bouncers, not like them yellow-bellied cowahds that lit out on youh when you needed 'em most. And these new boys is all ahmed and dang'rous. And youh 'sperienced at handlin' drovahs, we all are. It'll be all right, and youh'll make a potful o' money."

"Are you always so optimistic?"

"Allus. Allus look foh the silvah linin'. It's theah, but youh gotta look to find it. Come on, let's play . . ."

The Cockeyed Coyote was once again refurbished, resplendent and ready for the drover invasion. With the addition of Star Hopwell and the other three girls, the Muddy Springs locals began to take a fancy to the place. From early afternoon on, the bar was crowded with patrons, keeping Roy Pendleton and his new assistant busy. No one, however, not even the town poker regulars, seemed interested in daytime play.

The upright piano arrived and was ceremoniously installed in the bar. It would be at least another two weeks before the steel doors arrived. The hole in the ceiling that Perry had designed when the place was first revamped—a peephole a man stationed in the rafters could look down at the activity in the casino—was plugged.

"The way the last bunch shot up the room it's lucky we forgot to put our all-seeing eye up there. Somebody would have blown it through his head."

Horne sat at one of the poker tables shuffling, cutting, and dealing himself four hands of five-card stud. Perry's four female poker students wanted to test their newly acquired skills and had asked for a game of penny-ante with the boss. It was about 4:30 in the afternoon.

"Stay and watch," said Horne to Perry. "See how good a teacher you are. It should be fun."

"I can't. I'm riding out to Mary Alice's. She invited me to supper."

"Did she? Is something going on I don't know about?"

"I brought her a little present in lieu of flowers. There is no florist in this burg." He produced a small package wrapped in white tissue paper and tied with a pretty pink bow.

"Candy?"

Perry shook his head. "Mechanics Delight Dark Navy double-thick plug tobacco. It's her favorite."

"Sorry I asked. Tell her to brush her teeth before she kisses you good night."

Perry glided off, passing the four girls coming in. Francine-Mae, the redhead with the mole, carried a small sack that Horne deduced must be full of pennies. He had not played penny-ante poker since he was a boy when he, Perry, and a couple of Perry's boardinghouse acquaintances took a fling at it. At the time he'd only been eleven or twelve; Perry had encouraged him to play. He maintained that even playing for matches was excellent practice, as long as the players took the game seriously and did not alter their usual style of play simply because real money wasn't involved.

Horne rose from his chair to greet the girls. Francine-

Mae sat across from him, Star to his right; Eula-Mae—a platinum blonde from St. Joseph, Missouri, who claimed to have been married six times and was only twenty-three— sat between Star and Francine-Mae; and Ora-Mae, a willowy brunette with a come-hither mouth and eyes, lovely face, and creatively crafted padding to conceal a chest so flat as to be almost concave, sat between him and Francine-Mae to his left.

"We'll pretend the pennies are dollahs, T.G.," announced Star. "Okay?"

"Fine with me."

Each one bought a dollar's worth of pennies to start and Horne dealt for the deal. The jack of spades fell to Francine-Mae and she elected seven-card stud. Compared to bridge, poker was an easy game to learn. It became intricate only if the player wanted to play well. Play well and one cannot help but win, despite pulling one's share of poor hands, losing out by a hair to slightly better hands, and occasional disastrous nights. Play well and you can't help but win because most amateurs do not play well, do not master the odds, do not know when to stay or drop. They do not know how to bluff successfully, and fail to note and remember discards and have no patience.

The game was not four hands old before Horne decided that Perry had taught his pupils well. All four had yet to master the finer points of the game, but they seemed to know the value of their respective hands, when to bet, when to fold.

Their unanimous favorite was not one of his: spit-in-the-ocean. Each player was dealt four cards, and one final card was dealt faceup in the center. The faceup card was wild, as were the other three cards of the same value. Hands tended to be fantastically high, with four of a kind the average winner. Occasionally, a full house would collect the pot, but flushes and straights were worthless.

Horne generally avoided all wild-card games, except draw, five- and seven-card stud, which included the cuter, the joker; of value only with aces, straights, and flushes. Three of every four hands in this game were spit-in-the-ocean. The wild card inflated the value of everybody's hand, quickly becoming boring, and he politely asked if they could stick to straight draw and the two studs.

"Those are the games the customers will want to play most of the time, the games you'll want to become really good at. Remember, the house gets a five-dollar playing fee from every player and takes ten percent of the winners' profits. What does that signify to you, Francine-Mae?"

"Cockeyed Coyote makes money?"

The others giggled and laughed.

"It does, but what I'm getting at—"

Ora-Mae spoke up. "The better we play the game, the less the others win, the smaller the ten percent."

"Exactly. Very good, Ora-Mae. So always play just good enough to belong in the game, but don't ever try to clean anybody's clock. And remember how much each of the winners wins. They'll expect you to ask them at the end of the game."

"What if they fib?" asked Star.

"They can't, not very well. The other players, especially the losers, will take exception, jump in to correct them. Always look for at least one big winner and possibly one or two others who come out ahead. They're the source of our ten percent, two percent of which you get. What the house is doing is making money on the shift; the amount that shifts from one player to another. It's my deal. What do you say to seven-card stud?"

They played steadily for upward of an hour and a half. The closed door muffled the babbling and occasional laughter out front. The game quickly took on a serious aspect. Anyone kibitzing, not seeing it was penny-ante, would have assumed the stakes to be sky high. Perry had done his job well; not one of the four played poorly; all showed patience and, to varying degrees, cleverness.

Nevertheless, he won everything in sight. The hands that came his way were stupendous. Four times in the hour and a half he drew four-of-a-kind natural. Full houses became ordinary; once he drew a straight flush to the king. Only three times did his hand slip below three of a kind in value.

In nearly twenty years of poker he had never seen such

a string of consistently high cards—in penny-ante, no less.
It began to grate on his nerves. What was he doing, he
thought, but squandering precious luck on a child's game?
Had each penny been ten dollars, by now he'd be flirting
with thirty or forty thousand. Luck was a liquid. Every
player in the game had his bottle; how full the bottle
became was strictly up to fate. At the moment his bottle
was overflowing. It gushed, it geysered. He won and won
and won and won. And sank deeper and deeper into the
doldrums. Frustration seized his throat and crinkled his
face in a scowl.

"Is something wrong, T.G.?" asked Star.

"What? Oh, no, nothing . . ."

"You look mad," said Francine-Mae.

He had just laid down five clubs and was reaching for
the pot: all forty-nine cents. His luck was uncanny. It was
miraculous. It was disgusting. It ravaged his mind, rattled
his nerves, and roiled his stomach. He fought down the
urge to rip the deck in half and fling it wide.

"Youh sure youh not mad?" asked Star.

"I'm not mad! I mean I'm not, I'm fine."

"You're winnin' evvythin' in sight," said Eula-Mae. "You
allus get such tremendous cards? You must be the luckiest man 'live. How much you think you've won?"

"At least seven or eight bucks," said Ora-Mae, eyeing his
tacks.

"Not that much," Horne said.

"Moah," said Star. "Youh got at least ten dollahs theah."

It was his deal. He opted for draw, jacks or better to
open. And promptly dealt himself honestly a pat heart flush.
It won handily, Eula-Mae, his only opponent, folding two
pair.

"Youh win again," sang Star gaily.

Happily for him, he assumed. He saw nothing happy
about it. It was fast becoming a nightmare. He suddenly
hated even touching the cards, despised the simple act of
nudging his ante toward the pot. The game was now
almost two hours old. He wanted out desperately, wanted
to jump up and rush out the door, but he couldn't make
himself look like a sore winner.

"Are youh okay, T.G.?" asked Star.

"Fine, fine."

"I've been keeping count," said Ora-Mae. "You've won eight of the last ten hands. You sure are some poker player. Do you ever lose?"

Before he could answer, fate smiled on him. The door opened. It was Roy. So happy was he at the interruption he wanted to jump up and hug him.

" 'Scuse me, Boss, but I'm goin' to supper. We're taking turns. It's pretty busy out front . . ."

Horne jumped up. "I'll help. Sorry, girls, that's it for me."

"But you've won all the money," bawled Eula-Mae.

"You four keep playing, it's good practice. You're doing just fine, great; you're all real fast learners. Keep it up and you'll be cardsharps before you know it. Here . . ."

Nearly three pounds of pennies rose in stacks in front of him. He pushed them in every direction. All four protested his generosity vigorously. He smiled and left.

It was nearing a quarter to seven. The crowd in the bar had begun to thin shortly after Horne tied on an apron and joined Roy in serving. Presently, only four patrons were drinking.

"It gets dead like this 'round suppertime evvy night," explained Roy.

"Why don't you go eat? I can hold the fort here. And Elliott should be back from supper soon."

"Aren't you hungry?"

"Not really. My stomach's a little churned up."

Horne didn't mind tending bar. It served a purpose other than relieving the two bartenders' burden. It placed him in a position to meet his clientele face to face. The customers liked that. One or two even commented that Albert Cutshaw had never tied an apron on as long as they'd known him.

He wondered where Cutshaw had gotten to. Probably not far; the poker game had all but broken him. What an impulsive thing to do; crazy! To bet anything but money you could afford to lose on a single poker hand was simpleminded.

*   *   *

The second wave of drovers hit town jut before noon the next day. All that the Cockeyed Coyote lacked was the two steel doors on order from Pittsburgh, but as things turned out, they weren't needed. Horne met the first group advancing on the place in front of the batwing doors. His six new bouncers, without exception powerful and mean-looking, lined up behind him, their arms folded so as to inflate their biceps, sporting their six-guns in plain sight. The girls, Roy, and Elliott stayed inside behind the bouncers. Perry found an even safer place to position himself for the occasion. When word arrived that the drovers were on their way into town, he climbed on his horse and rode out to Mary Alice's.

Star had fashioned a sign and nailed it to the door to the casino:

No Horses Allowed!
This Means Your Horse!

Sight of the armed muscle backing up the proprietor persuaded the drovers to accede to Horne's polite request to check their weapons at the door. The afternoon and evening turned out boisterous, peaceful, and highly profitable. At four in the morning Roy, Star, and Horne added up the take. It came to a whopping $2,142.40, plus a couple of Mexican coins sneaked under Roy's watchful but busy eye in payment for beer. A single unpleasant incident marred the drovers' visit. A fight broke out in the bar; one man smashed another against the brand-new piano, shattering the front and loosening a dozen keys. The man responsible was so drunk he could hardly stand over the one he'd knocked down, but his friends obligingly relieved his wallet of enough money to pay the damages.

Not a single drover had to be bounced.

Horne lay in bed alongside Star positively glowing with satisfaction. It came from two sources: his companion's most recent failure to resist his advances, and the gloriously profitable evening.

"I wonder how many more drives will be coming this way?" he mused aloud.

"Dozens, Ah bet. By the time they stop northerin' youh'll be a rich man. Ah'm so happy for youh, T.G."

"You're sweet. You know, Perry was right; Mary Alice, too: if you're properly prepared, you don't have to worry about a riot, danger, or damage. That bunch took one look at the bouncers and did as they were asked."

"Let's do it again," she murmured throatily.

"The sun's coming up."

"Ah see somethin' else comin' up . . ."

She laid hold of him, hardening him to full erection, then lay back, spread her quim with her fingers, and leered. Horne reached for his wallet on the nightstand, flipped open the change pocket with his thumbnail, got out a quarter, and dropped it into her cunt.

"What the . . ." She leapt from the bed and began jumping up and down, her huge breasts flaping loudly and bouncing fit to jump free of her chest. The quarter clattered to the floor.

"Just foh that, the shop's closed foh the night."

"Aw, Star, honey, I was only playing . . ."

"A quahtah! Youh coulda at least put in a ten spot."

"Okay, I'll put in a ten spot."

"Don't youh dare! Youh wanna piggy bank, Ah'll buy youh one; youh keep youh money outta me, y'heah?"

"I hear."

He grabbed and kissed her, holding her tightly, shoving his erection between her legs. She tightened her thighs, squeezing, vising it, sending pain lancing back to his gut.

"Owwwww!"

She let go, shrieked with laughter, and dropping to her knees, began eating him. Once begun, she refused to stop, even when he came. She swallowed it in one gulp without missing a stroke, continuing to suck, suck, suck. She got him hard again, he ejaculated again, and still she refused to let go.

"Hey, hey, hey, hey, hey. . ."

He planted both palms against her forehead to push her off. She pinched his rear end; he yelped, and on she sucked. And sucked. And sucked. The third time he came, he didn't. Nothing, not even air, came out, confirming his balls were as empty as an echo. There was no way she could get him hard a fourth time. Out of sympathy for his plight and disappointment at her own, she let him loose and back into bed they tumbled.

She fell asleep almost immediately. Despite being worn out, he was unable to, so worked up was he over the night's profit and the startling difference between the first herders' visit and this group's: the difference between a funeral and a wedding. He congratulated himself on his change of mind, his decision to stay in business.

Again he wondered what had happened to Cutshaw; wherever he'd gone, if he ever got wind of the Coyote's overnight success, he'd probably jump off the highest cliff he could find—after kicking himself blue. Why it had never occurred to him to convert the back room into a gambling casino, particularly when he was already holding poker games there, was a mystery. Maybe he was too cheap to hire more help, too cheap to spend the money to fix the place up. Maybe he was just shortsighted. Many people in business are. Horne could thank his stars that he wasn't one of them.

Continuing to glow, reveling in the knowledge that he had conquered not one, but two worlds—professional gambling and business—he felt his eyelids grow heavy. And still gratification warmed him, so proud was he of himself. He was developing roots in the community; the Coyote would build his fortune; he would live comfortably, perhaps marry, raise a family, and best of all, hold his head high as a success.

What a beautiful, what a splendid, spectacular future beckoned!

8

Horne was tending bar the next evening by himself, waiting for Star and the other girls, when a man came in and stood at the bar. Horne put him at about fifty, lean, wiry, rugged-looking, a man who'd been through the mill, emerging unscathed, unruffled, unimpressed by the experience.

" 'Evening," said Horne. "What's your pleasure?"

"Scotch."

Horne served him, setting the bottle alongside his tumbler.

He sipped and glanced about. "Nice-looking layout. Looks like it's all been redone."

"It has."

"Very nice." He sipped. "Albert around?"

"Albert?"

"Cutshaw."

"Oh," said Horne, "he's left town. I think he has. I haven't seen him around lately. I'm sure he's gone."

"That's funny. What would he be doing walking out and leaving the Coyote?"

"He didn't exactly leave it. By the way"—Horne extended his hand—"T. G. Horne."

"Addison Kimbell."

"Welcome to Muddy Springs."

"Thanks. It's been a long time, years and years."

"You've been here before?"

71

"Twelve years ago. Did I understand you to say Albert didn't exactly leave the Coyote? What does that mean?"

"He lost it in a poker game. To me. We were both holding spade straight flushes. Two natural spade flushes in the same hand, can you imagine? Mine was to the queen. He bet the Coyote and lost."

"Did he really? That's wild."

"I thought it rather bizarre myself."

"That's not what I was referring to." Kimbell took another sip of his Scotch and set it down. He hard-eyed Horne. "I don't understand how he could bet the Coyote on a poker hand or anything else. When it didn't even belong to him."

"Oh, it did; he owned it, all right."

"Like hell he did." Again he paused and sipped.

"Mister . . ." began Horne.

"Addison Kimbell, friend. The Coyote wasn't Albert's. Ever. It belongs to me, every board, every nail, even the land it stands on. I left town, left Albert in charge. I went down to South America: Bolivia. Been down there mining tin all this time. I wrote to him every so often; he'd answer. On average about once a year. Neither of us was very good at writing letters.

"As I say, he was in charge; hired and fired, kept the bar stocked, the swinging doors oiled."

"Now wait a minute. He held the deed; it was in his name only and he bet it on that hand. He showed it to us. I read it, every word. His name was on it: Albert B. Cutshaw."

"Albert F. for Francis. And it couldn't have been his name you saw, it was the initials A B C. Not Albert B. Cutshaw, just plain A B C for the A B C Management Company. That's me, friend, I own this place, one in Milan, another in South Haven. All three: A B C. It sounds to me like our mutual friend put one over on you." He drank, emptying his glass. And refilled it.

"There must be some mistake," said Horne, unable to suppress the edge of desperation in his tone.

"There sure is, and you've made it."

Horne turned and took down the framed deed from the

wall alongside the mirror. When he turned back to the
bar, Kimbell had gotten out his wallet and brought out two
well-worn pieces of paper folded in quarters. He carefully
unfolded one, then the other.

"This is the deed. Notice the date. This is the bill of sale
for the land I got from Henry Templeton. I put up the
building."

Horne studied both documents for a long time before
speaking. By the time he did, panic had taken hold of his
heart and he could feel the nerves at the back of his neck
tighten.

"This is insane," he murmured, without—unfortunately—
even a slight trace of confidence in his voice. "I suggest
we both go sit down with Paul Flanagan."

"Who's he?"

"My lawyer. He drew up this deed of ownership. He can
straighten this all out."

Kimbell sipped. He eyed Horne quizzically. "What's to
straighten out? You can read English, can't you?"

"It's almost six o'clock. I'll close up, we'll go over to
Paul's office."

"You. There's no need for me to tag along. It's your
problem." Horne reached for the two documents on the
bar. Kimbell flattened a hand over each of them. "I'll hang
on to them. I wouldn't want anything to happen to them,
would I?"

The doors opened; it was Roy and Elliott. Horne glanced at
them, then at Kimbell, then back to them. There was no
hint of recognition in the eyes of any of the three.

"I'll be back," said Horne.

"Take your time, I'm not going anyplace. Now that I'm
home at last."

Attorney Paul Xavier Flanagan's office was a pack rat's
nest, piled with folders, legal records, documents, and
other dust gatherers of the lawyer's calling. His flat-topped
desk was approximately twice the size of an orange crate.
A single Palladian window that looked as if it hadn't been
washed inside or out since it was installed, admitted just
enough light from the dying sun to set Flanagan's pink

pate gleaming. He was a small man, middle-aged, astigmatic, perpetually harried, a man driven by his low self-esteem to labor fourteen hours a day six days a week, untangling legal knots for himself and skillfully tangling them for his colleagues in the trade. He never seemed to smile, but then—Horne had decided when he first met him—he had little reason to: no wife, no family, few friends, mostly other lawyers, no hobbies, no clubs or other group activities, nothing but work.

"I wish I could see his deed and bill of sale," he said to Horne upon hearing about the situation, "but actually it doesn't matter."

"What does that mean?" Horne asked warily.

On his way over to the office the worm of panic that had eaten its way into his heart with Kimbell's appearance felt as if it had given birth to myriad butterflies, migrating en masse to his stomach.

"If they're properly signed, dated, and notarized, they've got to be legal as hell."

"Not with Cutshaw's superseding them. Kimbell says Albert's name didn't appear on the deed he gave me. Only the letters A B C for A B C Management Company. But I swear I saw Albert's name on that deed."

"I never laid eyes on it, so I can't help you there."

"I saw it, I tell you."

"Did you hang on to it?"

"No. Why would I? I certainly didn't expect somebody'd show up and question its validity. But don't you have a copy?"

"I didn't handle the deal for Albert. Besides, even if I did, I make it a firm rule not to keep copies of anything, certainly not property deeds. If I filed copies of everything I work on, I'd have to rent a warehouse. Look at this cubbyhole. There isn't room to swing a damn cat. I don't have a copy of his deed or yours."

"Good God . . ."

"Don't despair. This Kimbell could be trying to pull a fast one. Cutshaw's lit out for Lord knows where, Kimbell knows it; he can feed you six different flavors of horseshit without worrying about Cutshaw, or likely anybody else in this town, calling him on it."

"The trouble is he did have a deed and bill of sale."

"Which could be phony. On second thought, I really should take a look. Let's go back to the Coyote." Desperation and defeat had settled over Horne like two buzzards perching on his shoulders. "Don't look so down. If worse comes to worst, you'll just have to go looking for Cutshaw. I'm sure he hasn't taken off for Australia. He can straighten it all out for you."

"He can't straighten a damned thing if he did pull a fast one, and more and more I'm beginning to believe that's exactly what he did. I mean, if he was the legitimate owner of the Coyote, after he lost it, why would he leave town?"

Flanagan shrugged his narrow shoulders. "To get a fresh start? Change of scenery? Even just to get away from the site of the biggest disaster of his life. I know if it were me, I wouldn't want to walk past the Coyote every day knowing I'd lost the goddamn place in a game of stud. That's pretty tough meat to chew and swallow. Come on."

Horne, Flanagan, and Addison Kimbell repaired to the casino for privacy. Roy and Elliott busied themselves behind the bar serving the early-evening patrons. Horne and Kimbell sat on either side of Flanagan while the little man went over both documents.

"Look," said Kimbell, "we can straighten this all out in five minutes. All we have to do is get a hold of Henry Templeton. He'll back me up. He'll tell you he sold me the land. And my lawyer was Eugene . . . something."

"Fischer," said Flanagan.

"That's it."

"Gene Fischer's dead, and so is Henry. A lot of years have gone by. People do tend to die, especially the older ones."

"Do you see anything wrong with either paper?" Kimbell asked. "Anything phony or illegal?"

"No."

"That settles that, then."

"Not exactly," said Flanagan. "I'd say both of these are authentic, but Cutshaw's could be, too. How do we know you left him here to manage the place? How do we know you didn't sell out to him?"

"I didn't. There's no proof I did, no papers, nothing." Kimbell stared at Horne. "The deed he gave you simply wasn't his to give. Which was why he was so freehanded with it."

"Wait a minute," said Horne. "Why two deeds?"

Kimbell eyed him. "What do you mean?"

"I know what he means," said Flanagan. "If, as you say, you left Cutshaw in charge and left the deed to the place in the safe, what are you doing with a second deed?"

"Who says it is?" Kimbell glanced from one to the other, his expression indulgent to the point of patronizing. "You're reaching for straws, boys. This is no second deed, it's a copy of the original. Word for word. That should be easy enough for you to check."

"Is it word for word a copy?" Flanagan asked Horne.

"I don't know," said Horne lamely. "I . . ."

"You threw the one I left behind with Cutshaw away," said Kimbell.

"Why keep it? Would you?"

"I'm not the one who needs it now, friend. Look, I'm human, I can understand that all this comes as a great shock to you, and I sympathize. To have some stranger walk in the door and claim your property is theirs and show you legal proof can't be very pleasant, but that's the way it is. I'm the legal owner of this place, have been for fourteen years and will be for fourteen more. If you don't think so, we'll take it to court. Or you can back off here and now. You'd be saving yourself a lot of headaches if you do, but of course I can't decide for you."

"Mr. Kimbell . . ."

"Call me Ad, T.G., everybody does."

"I'll make it short; I smell a very big, very pungent rat. I think you're trying to pull a fast one. You found out as soon as you hit town that Albert had left. Anybody in town could have told you he'd lost the Coyote to me in the game. You knew Henry Templeton and Fischer are dead, so neither one can contradict your claim. You heard the place had turned into a gold mine practically overnight. You hung on to your original deed and bill of sale all these years the way lots of people keep old papers squirreled away. Now you think you can cash in on them at my expense—"

"I know I can, T.G. Tell you what I'll do, you step out of the picture, just as any judge in the state is going to order you to and I'll do right by you. Nobody's ever accused me of being heartless."

"Let me guess, you're going to offer me a job."

"You know how to tend bar."

"We already have the two best bartenders in town. They don't need me."

"Suit yourself, maybe there's something else you can do. Boys, I'll be on my way." He folded both documents, restored them to his wallet, and got up. "If either of you want me for anything, I'm staying at the Sunflower Hotel. T.G., I'll give you forty-eight hours to clear out. If you're not out by seven o'clock day after tomorrow I'll be forced to get a court order to evict you. And if necessary, the marshal to enforce it. Good day, gentlemen."

And he was gone. Roy and Elliott looked in. Through the open door Horne could see that a number of patrons had come in.

"Either of you ever see that fellow before?" Horne asked. They shook their heads and eyed him as if expecting explanation. "It's okay, you can go back to work."

The door was closed.

"I'm going to fight him every step of the way," said Horne.

"Every step you'll need a leg to stand on," said Flanagan dryly.

"Forty-eight hours to find Cutshaw."

"Don't worry about that. You don't have any deadline. As things stand, with both of you claiming ownership, it's a Mexican standoff. I'll get out my buggy, run on over to the county seat, and get hold of Adrian Coombes, Judge Coombes. Get a court order to padlock the place. Close up until you're prepared to present your side and you and Kimball can go head to head."

"I can't do that until I locate Cutshaw. That may take weeks. Damnation, why do these things always happen to me? I've got to start looking right away. Tonight. Do me a favor, when you get back from Wellington, stop off at the widow Tubbs. Perry'll be there; he's practically moved in. Tell him the whole story. Tell him I've left town."

"Wait, wait, wait. For where? You have no idea where Cutshaw's gotten to."

"Somebody around here must know."

"Maybe he didn't tell anybody; if he did pull a fast one on you, why would he divulge where he's heading?"

"He might; after all, he had no way of knowing Kimbell would show up after all these years."

"You can't be absolutely sure of that, either. They could be in cahoots."

"Oh, my God, you think so?"

"I said they could."

"I'll cross my fingers they're not. I'm going to make the rounds, talk to Albert's friends, the boys in the game that night. They know him as well as anybody."

"He and Jake Farnsworth were pretty thick."

"Okay, I'll see him first. Then Culkin, Amos Darling, Toricelli . . ."

He went to the door and called Roy back in.

"What's up, Boss?"

"I'm leaving town. I have no idea how long I'll be gone, but tomorrow morning the place'll be closed up. Put a sign on the door: closed till further notice. When the steel doors get here, put them up. Until they do, nail some boards across the front and back doors."

"What the hell is goin' on?"

Horne turned to Flanagan. "Tell Perry I said everybody's to be paid their wages while we're closed. No matter how long we are. Tell him I'll be in touch from wherever I light. Tell him everything. I'll be seeing you both."

"Good luck, son," said Flanagan. "Find him, he's your ace in the hole. If Kimbell's a phony, he'll tell you so; if he's on the up and up, if he, Cutshaw, did the hornswoggling, you'll find out. If that proves to be the case, he owes you the value of this place plus the money you put in for improvements."

"The son of a bitch is broke."

"How do you know that?"

"Why bet the Coyote? He sure was tapped out at the table."

"Maybe he bet the Coyote because he thought he held the winning hand. A lot of poker players are creatures of impulse. I shouldn't have to tell you. Just because he bet it is no reason to assume it was all he had. T.G., don't even start trying to figure the thing out until you talk to him. He's got all the answers. Go talk to his friends, get on your horse, and go find him. *Vaya con Dios.*"

9

On the way to the stable, Star passed through his roiling thoughts; he didn't have time to say good-bye, but she'd understand. He only hoped Perry would. Flanagan was right: a powerful promising poker hand could turn the most cautious player into an impulsive plunger. He'd seen it happen. And Albert's style wasn't exactly conservative.

Damn but he wished he'd hung on to the old deed! No use groaning over it now. Hindsight and two cents would buy you a two-cent stogie.

Addison Kimbell. A cool one. If he *was* running a con, he was very good at it. Practiced. Never raised his voice, as calm as they come, the perfect gentleman. People dealing from strength generally are. Knowing you're on solid ground always breeds confidence.

He'd love to discuss the situation with Perry before leaving, but there was no time for that either; besides, he'd probably try to discourage him from going, criticize it as a wild-goose chase. Still, what alternative did he have? Without Albert he couldn't prove a damned thing. Kimbell's deed and bill of sale would stand straight and tall in court and he'd wind up with the losing hand.

No.

The Coyote was his; aside from the money he'd invested and the toil, he'd already put his blood into it. It was his future, everything he'd ever wanted. It was stability, security. Never again tar and feathers, no more fleabag hotels or rotten meals or passed-up rotten meals for want of the

price. No more streaks of rotten luck, no more running
from town to town; relief at last from the hazards of the
trade. Strangers' threats, guardians of civic virtue, the
law. If business kept up the way it was going, he'd quit
playing altogether. Put his deck and skills away permanently. Shelve his wits and rely on his intelligence and
charm.

Perry would love that. He'd snort and scoff and belittle;
still, he could do it. Gambling was no disease with him,
only a job. Once established as a businessman, he'd never
have to turn another card. If Perry couldn't buy that, too
bad for him.

He came within sight of the stable. Jake Farnsworth sat
in a chair tilted against the front, squinting at a newspaper,
moving his lips with every syllable.

"Howdy."

Horne asked him about Albert.

"Albert," murmured Farnsworth; a trifle nostalgically,
thought Horne, as if he already missed his friend. "He
didn't leave town the day after the game, y' know. It wasn'
till three or four days later."

"Any idea where he's gone?"

"Could be anywheres; didn' say. He did stop by to say
good-bye, and I ast. I 'member he said he wasn' sure, jus'
wanted to get out. Hey . . ."

"What?"

"Did you know he was keepin' comp'ny with a widder
over to Chatauqua County? Been frien's with her for ages.
I 'member him sayin' she was loaded."

"Where in Chatauqua County?"

"Cedar Vale, I think he said. No, by gum, it was further
east: Sedan. That's it, Sedan. But that ain' sayin' he
headed there."

"He was pretty smitten with this widow?"

"Hell, yes. Showed me her pitcher onc't. Fine figger of
a woman, purty face. I 'member him sayin' she was a
hardshell Baptis. Husban' died long time back, left her
comfor'ble. Real comfor'ble."

"What's her name, do you remember?"

"Lemme think. French, I think it was. De somethin'."

"What? Think. I have to find him, it's terribly important."

"How can you be sure he went ovah there?"

"It's a start. De . . . what?"

"French. Channey, Choise . . . I don' 'member." He frowned, then brightened. "But her fust name was Ag'tha. Or was it Anto'nette? Coulda been Ab'gail."

"It begins with A."

"I think."

"Try to remember, please."

"I'm tryin'. Ad'line? Ange? I can't 'member."

"Okay, thanks anyway. For trying."

"If you do find him, say 'lo for me."

"I will."

Byron Culkin was even more help, albeit in a different direction.

"I figured he was going for good when he drew all his money out of the bank."

"He had a bank account?"

"A very healthy one. Around fifteen thousand."

"Fifteen!"

"That surprises you?"

"I thought he was broke. He was just about busted when he put the deed to the Coyote into the pot."

"Oh, that's Al all over. Deal him a strong hand and he falls in love with it. Bets it to the hilt. He figured he had a sure winner. Two natural spade flushes in the same hand—amazing."

"He could have called me with an IOU. You'd have backed him up."

"I would have. He was good for it, all right; maybe he figured you wouldn't accept it. Or my word it was good, you being a stranger, us two friends. I don't know what was in his mind. He wasn't the easiest chap to figure."

"How long did he own the Coyote?"

"Years and years."

"Ever hear the name Addison Kimbell?"

"Kimbell, Kimbell . . ." Culkin's brow corrugated. He was unquestionably more intelligent than Jake Farnsworth, younger, sharper, better memory. "Who is he?"

"Just hit town. Walked into the Coyote and claimed he owns it. Never sold it to Albert; they were friends, he left town, left Albert to manage the place."

"I don't believe it. Al bought it . . . Kimbell, I think from him. It's been a long time."

Horne told him about Kimbell's deed and bill of sale.

"Sounds to me like you need a lawyer."

"Paul Flanagan's working on it for me, but I've got to track down Albert. He's the only one that can clear it up. I understand he has a lady friend over in Sedan."

"I heard he did, although not from him. I don't recall who told me."

"Do you remember her name?"

"I never heard it. If anybody'd know, it'd be Jake. He was just about his best friend. If you do catch up with him, be sure to give him my best, would you?"

"Sure. You've been a big help, Byron, appreciate it."

"I have? You could have fooled me."

"One last question. Would you say Albert was straight arrow?"

"Far as I know. But he was a private man, the sort who only tells you so much about himself and no more."

"You think he's capable of cheating me? Not owning the Coyote and making me think he did?"

Culkin thought for a long time, then didn't actually answer the question. "It's possible. I can't honestly answer that. I always assumed he owned it, we all did. No reason to think otherwise. Maybe he didn't. Maybe he'd been in charge so long he came to feel in his heart he really did own it. He could certainly afford to buy it."

"How did he make his money?"

"I don't know that either; but as long as I've known him, he's had money. Don't forget to give him my best."

Albert may have had money, but calling with a deed that didn't belong to him was a clever way of getting out of tapping his bank account. A chilling thought traversed Horne's mind as he walked away from Culkin's house. *Had* Albert flimflammed him and was the whole town in on it?

That was stretching things more than a bit. The fewer people in on any flimflam, the better its chances for success. He visited Hugh Toricelli and Amos Darling; neither could add very much of substance to what Farnsworth and Culkin had already told him. However, Darling did mention that Albert left town to go to Wellington on average every other week and was usually absent at least three days.

Maybe that's where he'd gotten to. First he'd check out Sedan, then Wellington. Sedan, the county seat of Chatauqua County, lay about eighty miles east of Muddy Springs. He stopped three times to rest his horse. By the time the sun came up over the Ozark Plateau dead ahead, every bone ached in man and horse. Shortly after eight in the morning, he rode into Sedan. It was four times the size of Muddy Springs, neater, more pleasing to the eye, most of the houses and many buildings painted white. In evidence was something sadly lacking in Muddy Springs: community pride. Even the residents themselves looked sprucer, better dressed, for the most part socially superior to those of Muddy Springs.

A sign affixed to the front of a new one-story building caught his eye: C. Abel Tewes—Sheriff.

He found the law feet up on the desk, his boots side by side beside his chair. He couldn't have been much more than forty, but looked fifteen years older. Exhausted, frazzled, unshaven, as if he'd been up all week. He was dozing when Horne walked in. A fly buzzed around his head, its drone accompanying his soft snoring.

"Ahem!"

Sheriff Tewes bolted awake blinking furiously, scowling, softening his stubbled features and questioning Horne with his eyes.

Horne apologized for awakening him and introduced himself. "I'm looking for a friend. It's possible he's visiting here in Sedan."

"Visiting who?"

"I'm not sure of her name. It's French, I think. De . . . Antoinette De . . ."

"You don't mean Aveline Del Cassé?"

"Could be."

"What's your friend's name?"

"Albert Cutshaw."

"Cutshaw. Tall, well-built, red hair? Growing a beard?"

"Sounds like him. You know him?"

"I'd sure like to meet him."

"I don't understand."

"You say you think he was visiting Miz Del Cassé?"

"I'd hope to find him at her place."

"You won't. Her either. Turn around and look out the window."

A funeral cortege was passing slowly. "That's her."

"Oh, my God . . ."

"She was murdered at her house out on the Peru road two days ago. A couple neighbors spotted your friend Cutshaw riding away from the scene of the crime hell-bent for leather. Unless it wasn't him. But redheaded fellows aren't that common around here. Me and the boys been out beating the bushes looking for him the past two days and nights."

"You really think he murdered her?"

"Somebody did. Broke her neck. If we catch him, he'd best come up with a damned good alibi. Aveline Del Cassé was one fine lady. Widow. Lived alone. Knew everybody for miles around, friendly with everybody, good churchgoer, always ready with a helping hand. She's sure gonna be missed around here. I got to know her well, my pleasure. I'd be at her funeral now if one of the boys'd get back and hold the fort for me. I'm not supposed to close the office during working hours, you know, state law." He sighed. "I'm getting too old for this job. I'm forty-two, and that's old. I don't get a kick out of it like I used to. Takes too much out of a man.

"My mother wanted me to be a dentist. Can you imagine? I even went to dental school up in Ellsworth. Lasted two weeks. Couldn't take it, couldn't stand the sight of bloody teeth.

"Any ideas where Cutshaw might have headed? I'd appreciate any help you can give us." Tewes was staring appealingly.

"I'd like to help, but Sedan's about the only town I've been able to connect him with. He came over from Muddy Springs."

"I thought like everybody else, sitting in the dentist's chair getting teeth pulled was rough. Let me tell you, standing over it doing the pulling is twice as bad. Murdered her, stole her money. We found the floor torn up in the bedroom and her strongbox with the lock busted empty. I don't know why in hell people keep big money at home with two perfectly good, safe banks in town."

"I can't believe Albert did it."

"He was seen riding away from there."

"I know, but when he left, she could still have been alive."

"That's true. If we could only talk to him. If you catch up with him before we do, I advise you to do the right thing by the law. There's an arrest warrant out, and aiding and abetting a murder suspect is pretty risky. Plain stupid. If you do catch up with him, you'll be doing him a favor if you talk him into giving himself up. He'll be treated fairly—my word on that."

"I understand."

"Aiding and abetting a murder suspect could land a man behind bars himself. I don't have to draw you pictures."

"I said I understand."

"Blood spurting from peoples' mouths, the groaning, the agony in their eyes, their fear when they walk in, I couldn't take any of it. I've got twenty-three men out: ten deputies, thirteen volunteers. After the funeral half the able-bodied men in town'll be out searching. We'll no doubt find him before you do. Unless there's something you're not telling me."

"I've told you everything I know. Have a nice day."

Tewes didn't hear. He had dropped off again. Back came the fly to pester. Horne stood outside. The funeral cortege had moved two blocks up the street, heading out of town for the cemetery he'd passed on his way in. Two boys walked by, pushing and shoving each other playfully.

"Which way to the Peru road, fellows?" One pointed.

"You wouldn't happen to know the Del Cassé house, would you?"

"That's the one with the all-red barn, red roof and all. About two miles out."

He did want to get started as soon as possible, but common sense prevailed over impetuosity. He walked his horse to the nearest stable to rest and feed, then walked himself to a diner for breakfast. He decided he would catch a few hours' sleep before starting his search, suspecting that once he began, it might take him into nightfall, possibly even through the night without sleep, the second night in a row.

He took a hotel room and left a call for four hours later. It was 1:30 in the afternoon when he came back out. During his nap the day had changed dramatically. It had been a beautiful morning flooded with sunshine and capped by a cloudless blue sky. Now the sky was gray with clouds surrounding an enormous black-bellied one, and it was as dark as after twilight, just before night sets in. He got his horse and set out for Aveline Del Cassé's.

He recognized the all-red barn from a good mile distant. Sight of the house as he drew closer, the little picket fence, the gate standing ajar invitingly, the profusion of colors among the flowers neatly arrayed across the front on either side of the steps, the immaculate whiteness of the place could not prevent an eerie feeling from invading his heart. The house looked deserted and ominous, forbidding. Set against the dour sky, the menacing clouds, it appeared to threaten, to warn him to stay away. Lightning split the clouds, thunder grumbled.

Was the house in mourning for its murdered mistress? Could it feel its loss, the brutality of it? Was it summoning its resentment against his, a stranger's intrusion at such an inopportune time? He consciously suppressed a shudder.

Why was he visiting it? What could he expect to find inside that would help him find Albert? He would know when he found it if he did. He led the horse into the barn. He wasn't ten steps from the front door when the storm struck. Lightning ripped the sky, briefly bluing the landscape, detonating thunder. The rain came hurtling down in buckets. Up to the door he rushed. He half-expected to see a sign of some sort forbidding trespassing tacked to the door by Sheriff Tewes. There was none. The door was unlocked.

Lightning brightened the parlor. The house looked very lived-in, enjoyed, carefully cared for, attractively, tastefully furnished. Rain pounded the roof like hail. He could not see through the windows so heavy was the downpour. A deluge. He'd been just in time getting under cover. Another ten seconds and he would have gotten soaked to the skin.

He went into the bedroom: Aveline's. The vanity was skirted with a red polka-dotted material, matching the curtains. An oval throw rug picked up the red, adding a dark blue in contrast. It covered the floor alongside the bed. The bed itself, covered with a tufted white spread, stood flush against the wall on the far side. Beyond the throw rug just in front of the closet door, the floor had been ripped up; it looked as if with a crowbar. A strongbox, its lock shattered, lay open and empty among the broken boards, confirming Tewes' assertion that whoever had killed Aveline Del Cassé had done it for her money.

Examining the floor closely, T.G. found dried blood. He was kneeling, inspecting it, when he heard a sound out front that sent his hand to his .45. He drew, straightened, and flattening against the wall, turned slightly so he could see out front through the crack separating the upper and lower door hinges.

He gasped. A young girl had come in, clad in a flimsy cotton dress, sopping wet, that clung to her and he could see through. She was carrying a berry bucket. She came two steps into the parlor, then turned around and went back out, partially closing the door. Through the ruffled curtain covering the door glass he could see her silhouette as she held one hand over part of the top of her bucket, to keep the berries from spilling while she poured the water out. She set the bucket down and came back in.

He holstered his gun and went into the parlor. At sight of him she half-screamed, her hand to her mouth cutting it off.

"You scairt the daylights outta me!"

"I'm sorry. I wasn't expecting anybody."

"What you doin' here?"

"The same thing you are, I came in out of the rain."

"It's pourin' buckets."

She introduced herself: Joan C. Calhoun. Daddy wanted a boy. What daddy got was the furthest thing from one Horne had seen in ages. On she babbled in friendly fashion. He only half-listened, his concentration glued to her figure. Her thoroughly soaked dress covered nothing. Her breasts were large, beautifully formed. The nipples protruded firm and erect. His suddenly fascinated glance wandered down over her round little tummy to her vee. Her dark quim was clearly outlined; he easily envisioned the milky thighs bracketing it. Her hair hung limp, soggy and dripping. Her mouth was full, outrageously sensuous. She exuded sex in the way some women give off clouds of perfume. Every visible part of her blended beautifully, classically with every other. It was a body made in heaven, one of a kind, one of his lifetime.

"Wouldja get me a tollow?"

"A what?"

"A tollow, tollow, so's I can dry myself off."

"Oh, of course."

He retreated to the bedroom and into the bathroom. An oversize bath towel hung on the rack. He returned and handed it to her. The few seconds he was out of her sight she began to peel her dress off, unbuttoning the four buttons at the front and lifting it upward over her head. As innocently, as modestly as if she were removing her hat. Presenting herself mother-naked to his stranger eyes did not appear to ruffle her in the least. She didn't blush, didn't comment, gave no indication whatsoever of being even slightly inhibited. While all he could do was gape and swallow.

" 'Scuse me a sec."

Draping the towel over one arm, she returned to the front door, her lovely cheeks bouncing innocently, and wrung out her dress, returning with it, draping it over a chair back to dry. Then, posing in full view before him, she began to dry herself.

My God, he thought, what hath God wrought? Distractions, distractions.

"I was over by the crik berryin'. The bushes is the best there is there. I could see it was going to start, but I never dreamed it'd hit so powerful hard, so suddenlike. Buckets and buckets. I'll be lucky I don't catch my death of never git over. I poured the water outta my bucket; you don't think it'll rot my berries, do you? I mean so soon? Where 'bouts is Missus Delacosy?"

"Passed away, I'm afraid."

She stopped drying herself abruptly and stared at him out of her magnificent delft-blue eyes.

"Dead?"

"Murdered."

"Mercy me to goodness!" The twin blue skies widened. "Who woulda done such a horrible thing?"

"Nobody knows. Sheriff Tewes is investigating."

"Poor Missus Delacosy; she was so sweet, so kindly. Why would anybody wanta murder the poor thing?"

"Evidently for her money."

She finished drying and came forward, handing him the towel. "Do my back for me, please?"

He did so. When he was done she rolled her dress up in the towel, wrung it vigorously, and put the dress back on the chair.

"There we are; now I'm dry, it's not so chilly. You're lucky, you hardly got wet at all."

She set the heels of her hands against the sides of her breasts and pushed them together, jiggling them. He swallowed and died a little. She did it a second time, then flung her arms upward.

"I feel wonderful!"

Up on her toes she whirled around, swinging her arms, her breasts jouncing.

"Prickly. Warm and cozy, prickly here." She touched her nipples. "And down here." She swiped at her quim. "Like music is running through my whole body and coming out there. I can almost hear it. It feels soooooo good."

He was developing an erection; had his life depended on not erecting, he could not have prevented it. Harder and harder he grew, bulging his crotch conspicuously. And yet he couldn't move, couldn't tear his eyes from the vision before him. As he continued to swallow and stare, his heart pounding so it threatened to smash through his chest, her eyes drifted downward and came to rest on his bulge.

"Look . . . Look what you're doing."

"I beg your pardon," he murmured lamely.

She came to him and set her hand lightly against his bulge, then began to rub it. He backed away; she followed, continuing to play. He backed against the wall. She took away her hand. Less than four inches separated them. She moved her quim up flush against his cock, pressing hard and driving her breasts against his chest. Her arms went around his neck and she kissed him, thrusting her tongue deep, devouring him, sending golden needles shooting up from his crotch, lancing through his thundering heart, up his throat into his suddenly fevered brain, exploding, shooting in all directions.

He died.

He came alive in the bedroom; she had taken him by the hand and walked him in. He fumbled his clothes off awkwardly. She lay on the bed on her side, one knee drawn up, her great breasts pushed together from the weight of her left one, the nipples protruding fully half an inch, and sucking her thumb. At sight of his hard-on she stopped sucking. Her eyes widened with pleasure and she smiled.

"Mercy me to goodness, what a pretty, pretty pecker! It's even bigger than Claude Johnson's. Bigger than Everett Dreisward's. His brother Louis's, Kenny Castro's, the sheriff's, his deputies . . . Bigger than any boy's in the whole school. 'Most as big as Uncle Tol's; 'bout as big as the man who comes 'round in the spring to repair Maw's pots and pans, but nicer. Fatter than Henry Conklin's, too. I hate skinny peckers; it's like dropping a skinny stick into a mason jar; you can't keep it straight, it just rattles round. Elbert Castro, Kenny's brother's, is the skinniest pecker you ever did see. I like yours."

How old was she? he wondered. Old enough to take advantage of. Everybody seemed to; what right did he have to deny himself?

Her seemingly endless litany of conquering heroes finally came to its end when she took his cock between her lips and blew him. Whether she'd run out of names or only interrupted her list he had no idea. Until she resumed babbling after she was done, at the same time massaging him into a fresh erection.

He mounted her and thrust slowly forward. He pushed all the way in and was preparing to withdraw and begin pumping when to his astonishment and dismay, her cunt began to tighten, trapping his cock, rendering it impossible for him to withdraw. Vising it securely! Harder and harder she tightened, laughing gaily, teasing him, challenging him to pull free.

"Betcha can't, betcha can't. Nobody never can. I can tighten even more . . ."

"No no!"

"Feel it?"

"Ow, ouch! Stop, you'll break it! Please!"

She roared laughter and relaxed. "That didn't really hurt."

"It really did!"

"I just wanted to show you my trick power. You ever poke a gal who could tighten it tight like that before?"

"Never."

"I can tighten and hold you all night. I got extra strong muscles, stronger than anybody."

"I believe it."

"I won't do it again, I just wanted to show you."

"Right"

"You can start now."

"Thank you."

They fucked. That is he began, driving in somewhat hesitantly, his confidence that she wouldn't repeat her trick power not yet complete. He drew back halfway, whereupon she burst into song.

Oh, don't you remember sweet Betsey from Pike,
Oooo, ahhh . . .
Who crossed the big mountains with her lover Ike,
With two yoke of cattle, large yaller dog,
Ugh, mmmmm. Ohhh!
A tall shanghai rooster and one spotted hog.
Ahhhh, harder, harder, faster . . .
Singing tooral lal looral lal looral lal la,
Singing tooral lal looral lal looral lal la.
Ahhhhh, ahhhh, ahhhh
Singing tooral lal looral lal looral lal la,
Singing tooral lal looral lal looral lal la.
One evening quite early they camped on the Platte . . .

And on and on and on: all eleven verses, eleven choruses. He had never had intercourse with a woman who sang before. The novelty of it speedily wore off. He closed his eyes and tried not to listen, but her mouth was within inches of his ear, her voice high-pitched and slightly off-key, and he found it impossible to bar it from his hearing.

He fucked faster and faster, hoping he might exhaust her. All it did, however, was to inspire her to increase her own bucking and gyrating. One she sang:

A miner said, "Betsey, will you dance with me?"
"I will that, old hoss, if you don't make too free;
But don't dance me hard, do you want to know why?
Dog on you, I'm chock full of strong alkili!"

He good-naturedly joined her in the final chorus. With the last "la," she stopped fucking abruptly.

"What is it?" he asked.

"I'm plumb outta song. It's all over. How's about 'My Sweetheart's the Mule in the Mines'?"

"Whatever . . ."

"It's one of my special fav'rites."

It was followed by the "Young Man Who Wouldn't Hoe Corn" and "Seven-Cent Cotton and Forty-Cent Meat."

By the time they were done with both commodities, total exhaustion had set in. They lay side by side, Joan C. playing with his royal limpness. Then without warning, she jumped up and ran out into the parlor. He hauled on his trousers and joined her. She put on her dress. It was still wet enough to see through, but not sopping.

"It's stoppin' rainin', I got to go back to berryin'. 'Bye."

"Good-bye, Joan C."

She waved, started for the door, opened it, and turned around. "Can I ask you a question?"

"Ask away."

"What's your name?"

"James. James A. Harvey. Governor James A. Harvey." She wide-eyed him. "You're the governor?"

"That's me. I was on my way back to Topeka. I wandered a little out of my way."

"The governor!"

"Nothing to get excited about, really. In four or five years I plan to be president."

"President of the whole Yewnited States?"

"That's right. Five years from now if you ever get to Washington, look me up."

"Wowee! I will! I will!"

And she was gone.

Horne sighed, went back into the bedroom, and got dressed.

Joan C. Calhoun. Daddy wanted a boy. What he got was a hell of a lot more than he bargained for. From what he could see, three-quarters of the male population of Chatauqua county got more!

He began his search, starting in the bedroom. It struck him that Albert's extended trips to Wellington were more likely to Sedan, and he was fibbing to his friends to protect his love life from their needling. He'd come down here to this house. Had he murdered Aveline? Anything being possible, he could have. They could have had a lovers' quarrel. Stealing her money didn't seem like Albert, though; still, he really didn't know him. But he'd arrived there with plenty of cash of his own. To be sure, if you do murder somebody, for whatever reason, knowing a large amount of money is within reach, as knowing her he had to have known, the temptation might prove irresistible. There was always the rationalization, "What does she need with it now?"

He searched all her drawers and the cedar chest in the corner. Lastly, he searched the closet shelf. He found a number of shoe boxes. All except one contained shoes. In it was a packet of letters tied with a ribbon. He sat on the bed and untied the ribbon. All the letters were addressed to her in the same hand, a man's hand. Thirty-one showed Muddy Springs as the return address. The four exceptions all had the same return address: 1 Stapleton Street, Carl Junction, Missouri.

T.G. had heard of Carl Junction, although he'd never been there. It was a tiny bend in the road situated between Joplin and Webb City in the southwest corner of the state just over the border.

Did Albert have family there? He compared the dates on the postmarks of all four letters. They were dated various times of the year in consecutive years, including the present one. Evidently he went home to visit and wrote his Aveline from there. And was Carl Junction where he was heading when he rode away from the house two days before, when the neighbors spotted him and reported it to Tewes?

Or had he fled to Wellington? Had he fled at all? Or just left, his hands free of blood. He'd find out when he caught up with him. He opened the most recent letter from Carl Junction. he hesitated to read it, feeling a twinge of guilt. It was more than invading privacy; it was peeking through a keyhole into their bared souls. But he read it.

"My dearest darling Avvy,
Visiting father and Billy here in Carl Junction, as you can see by the postmark. Father's health getting worse, I'm sorry to say. The doctor's just about given up; he refuses to take his medicine and he coughs real bad nights. He's 82 and has lived a full life, but I hate to see sickness taking him. Seeing him waste away as he is. I miss you terribly as I always do. I'll be leaving here Mon-

day and will stop by to see you. It's over 200
miles so I'll be taking the train. Getting a little old
for horse and saddle that far. I'll be in some time
Monday early evening.

I do miss you. I know I already said that, but it
does wear something awful on me, being apart. I
think of you alone in that house with no one to
protect you, no one to even talk to. If we could
only be together all the time, for always. I know
how you feel about that and I respect it, but I live
for the day you'll change your mind. The day
you'll decide you need me as much as I need you.
I love you forever.

                                                   A

By the time T.G. got down to the initialed signature, he
felt even guiltier. And pitied Albert. And decided that no
man who felt so about a woman could possibly kill her.
Not in such a brutal manner. Unless she provoked him,
unless he couldn't take her rejecting him, had arrived at
the house tortured by memory of her previous refusals,
clinging to the hope that he could change her mind, failing
to, unable to stand it, losing his head . . .

He started on a second letter, one dated July of the
previous year, also sent from Carl Junction. He gave it up,
a tidal wave of shame flooding his conscience. He restored
it to its envelope, retied the packet, and put it back where
he'd found it.

Carl Junction, he thought as he left the house. Over two
hundred miles. Four hundred out of his way if he arrived
and Albert wasn't there. But that was a chance he had to
take. It had stopped raining; the sun had come out, bright-
ening the faces of the flowers along the front of the house
prettily. He rode back to town.

He returned to the hotel and asked the desk clerk if he
had any information on hotels in Missouri, specifically
Carl Junction. The man had no book he could consult, but
proved himself an enterprising sort.

"When you send your telegram to your friend, why not
just tell him to contact you care of the biggest hotel in

town. If he writes back or wires you, it ought to reach you right enough."

An excellent suggestion. He wired Perry telling him of his intention to continue on to Carl Junction, asking him to inform Flanagan. Describing Albert as "my elusive friend," he made it plain that he intended to chase him until he caught up. He did not mention the tragedy, saying only that he had good reason to believe that "my elusive friend" had gone to visit his family.

He made arrangements to stable his horses indefinitely, paying the stableman for two weeks' boarding. He boarded the 6:04 train to Coffeyville. There he was told he would be changing to Oswego, winding up in Joplin. No tracks connected Joplin to Carl Junction; he would have to rent a horse and ride nearly twenty miles north.

Sitting, watching Sedan slip out of his life, he thought about Joan C. Calhoun and poor Aveline Del Cassé, C. Abel Tewes and Albert. Had Albert ridden his horse all the way to Carl Junction? he wondered. If so he, Horne, would get there ahead of him. Albert couldn't possibly cover such a distance without stopping somewhere overnight, possibly even two nights. Lucky Carl Junction was so small; everybody in town probably knew him, definitely knew his family.

He wondered too about Addison Kimbell. Had Flanagan gotten the court order he seemed so sure he'd be able to get from the judge to close the Coyote until a decision as to the rightful owner could be reached? He must have by now. Good man, Paul Xavier Flanagan: shrewd, capable, reliable.

It was not yet seven when the train pulled into Coffeyville. The man who'd sold him his ticket in Sedan had told him there'd be a nearly two-hour wait in Coffeyville before his train to Oswego got in. He checked his saddlebags at the station and went sightseeing to kill time. The town was situated near the Verdigris River, about a hundred fifty miles south of Topeka.

He strolled by the C. M. Condon & Company Bank with its awninged upstairs windows and triangular roof mounts. He rounded the corner and his heart nearly stopped. Coming his way was none other than Albert Cutshaw. Albert recognized him, staring, glaring—as, Horne was sure, memory of their recent business dealings came to mind—relaxed into a grin, waved, and came forward.

"Richardson!"

"Albert."

"What the hell . . ."

"You first," said Horne good-naturedly. "What are you doing in Coffeyville?"

"I'm on my way to visit my family in Missouri.'

He neither looked nor behaved like a guilty man. His beard was about three quarters of an inch, and promised to be luxurious when fully grown. It was as fiery red as his hair.

"What are you doing here?" he asked.

"Following you."

"Me?"

"I picked up your trail in Sedan. You were seen leaving Mrs. Del Cassé's." He paused for effect. "After she was murdered."

Albert's jaw dropped; he gaped; his reaction was genuine; the news had astonished him.

"Murdered . . ." he repeated softly. "Avvy dead?"

"Her neck broken. Sheriff Tewes and his men are looking all over for you."

"He thinks I did it? That's crazy! I wouldn't harm a hair on her head. I loved her, she's the only woman I've ever loved. I was at her house, sure, but when I left, she was as alive as you are now. I never touched her. A broken neck. . ."

"Whoever did it stole her money."

"I didn't do it, man, I didn't!"

"Ssssh, calm down. I believe you."

"You better!"

"Tewes is the one you've got to convince. Can we go someplace and talk in privacy?"

They got a corner table in the rear of the small restaurant. Both ordered coffee. Shock was beginning to set in.

Albert listened white-faced to the few details Horne was able to provide him.

"Dead, murdered. I don't believe it." He covered his eyes and shook his head. "Poor Avvy. Poor, poor darling." He lowered his hands. "I swear by God almighty when I left there she was fine. We did argue, I admit, I . . . asked her to marry me. She turned me down like she always does. But I keep trying. The crazy thing is she wants to marry me; she does, I can see it in her eyes, the way she lowers her voice when she talks about it. She's afraid."

"Of what?"

"Not me. Of marriage. She's been alone so long since her husband died, she's used to it. Claims she is. Oh, she doesn't brood about it, nothin' like that. I think she keeps sayin' no, not 'cause I'm the one askin' her, only 'cause she's afraid to marry. You savvy what I'm tryin' to say?"

"I think I do. It would mean a big change for her."

"That's the whole thing. Oh, she hasn' said it in so many words, but that's it."

"Some people lose a loved one, fall in love with somebody else, but they're afraid to marry a second time, afraid they'll lose them, too. And don't think they can take such a blow a second time, it was so rough the first."

"That's it! You do understan'. I was there, I left. We argued, like I say, we were always arguin' over that, but there wasn't anythin' violent. I worshiped that woman. Adored her. I'd never harm her so help me. Whoever killed her musta come later."

"Killed and robbed her."

"Fuckin' bastard! If I ever find him, I'll blow his head off. Tewes suspect anybody?"

"You."

"Yeah, yeah, you said. Well, he's fulla shit!"

"Don't be too hard on him. He admits he doesn't have anything to go on except the neighbors seeing you leave the house."

"They're nuts!"

"They did see you."

"I didn't do it, I tell you!"

"Shhh. Of course not. But can I ask you something?

What are you doing here? You left Sedan two days ago. We're only four hours' ride from there."

"I've got friends here. I'm in no big rush. And I had things to do: get rid of my horse for one. I didn' plan to ride all the way to Carl Junction. Does that sound like a guilty man tryin' to get away?"

"Why didn't you get rid of your horse in Sedan?"

"I usually do—that is, I usually leave it with Avvy. But when I rode away from there, I was upset. Burnin'. I just wanted to ride and ride; you know, chew the wind for miles, get the frustration outta my system. Everybody sore about somethin' rides and rides it outta them, don't you?"

"You've been here two days and nights."

"I got here late afternoon day before yesterday. I was still boiling. Bought a couple bottles of Jefferson rye and got drunk as a hoot owl. I was sick to death the next day. Stayed in bed all day. Didn't leave the hotel till late this mornin'." He had an answer for every question, mused Horne. "What are you lookin' at me like that for. You don't believe me? It's the goddamned truth, every word!"

"If you say so. Actually, it doesn't really matter. Mrs. Del Cassé is not the reason I've been following you. It's the Coyote."

"What about it?"

They ordered a second cup of coffee. While they waited to be served, Horne told him about Addison Kimbell and his claim of ownership.

"He's fulla shit!"

"Ssssh. Albert, keep it down, please?"

"He's a damned liar. He sold me the Coyote back when. It was all legal as hell. He wanted out on account he was leavin' town."

"He went down to Bolivia."

"Bolivia?"

"South America. He says he's been down there all these years working tin mining."

"That's bullshit. He's never been to South America in his life. he left Muddy Springs to go out to Nevada to dig silver. Out east of the Simpson Park Mountains near Eureka. We wrote back and forth. He wasn' out there but about a year when he got into dutch. Some fella nearly beat him to death in a fight over a woman in a bar. That night the guy's friends found him dead. 'Thorities arrested Ad and put him on trial. He admitted to it. Can you believe it? I remember thinkin' when I heard, he's sure got balls to own up to murder. Only he claimed self-defense. And seein' the other fella had licked him before, the jury took it into consid'ration. Oh, they didn' let him off, but didn' hang him either. It fell somewheres between murder and manslaughter. He got ten years in the pen'tentiary in Carson City. Used to write me from there. Bolivia. What a buncha horseshit. If that ain't Ad all over."

"His deed and bill of sale looked authentic as hell."

"They're fake. Got to be."

"His lawyer's dead. There's no record of your buying the Coyote from him. He claims A B C Management is his company."

"Bullshit! It's mine. My daddy's 'nitials."

"Wait a minute. He also said he had other bars. One in . . . where . . . Milan!"

"There you go, that's easy enough to check. Check and see he's lyin' about that, you'll know he's lyin' about A B C. That's Ad all over. When he gets to bullshittin' and sees whoever he's talkin' to believes him, he goes overboard. Like all bullshitters."

"Nevertheless, he's got the documents, all I've got is you. A judge'll have to decide. I need your testimony, Albert. I'm willing to pay for your time and trouble to come back to Muddy Springs with me and tell your side of it. The truth. Between us maybe we can knock him down."

Cutshaw sucked a tooth, sipped his coffee, and eyed the backs of his hands.

"A thousan' bucks."

"Hey, that's pretty steep."

"That's my price. Chrissakes, you won the place with a goddamn poker hand, you oughta be willin' to spring for a few bucks to keep it."

"Okay."

They shook hands.

"When I come back from Carl Junction."

"Oh, no, right now. We start back today. We can take the train."

"Today okay, but no train. Not goin' through Sedan. Somebody could spot me easy and go runnin' to Tewes. We'll ride back and give Sedan a wide, wide berth."

"My horse is stabled back there."

"You can rent one here and, when we get back to Muddy Springs, have your horse brought over. And send somebody back here with a horse you rent, savvy?"

"I guess."

"A thousan' bucks."

"Paid in full when this mess is all cleared up."

"I'll clear it up, don' you worry. I can't wait to see old Ad's face when he sees me. Hot dog, he'll throw a conniption fit!"

10

They started back within the hour. Horne reflected on Kimbell's mention of owning a bar in Milan, another in South Haven, but decided that that was a lie that wasn't of much value to him. Confronted with it before a judge, Kimbell would only deny saying it.

One thing worried him: Albert was willing to testify in his behalf—for a price—but what good would it do him? He no longer had any material evidence that he'd purchased the Coyote from Kimbell. Henry Templeton, the lawyer was dead, and vanished were all records of the transaction.

"If you're worried it's gonna' come down to his word 'gainst mine, stop worryin'," said Albert. "I can trump any card the son of a bitch plays."

"How?"

"There's a copy of the bill of sale. Not the deed, but the bill of sale is all we need."

"Where?"

Albert winked and smirked. "Squirreled away where nobody but me can find it. I'll get it soon as we get back."

"Why so secretive? Aren't we partners?"

"That we are, but it's the thousan' bucks makes us. If I tell you where the bill of sale is, you'll be home free. You won't need me."

"I wouldn't do that to you, Albert."

"I don' believe you would, but there's no harm in my playin' safe."

"How is it you kept a copy of the bill of sale and not of the deed?"

"Oh, I had both. Henry Templeton drew up copies for me, only I mislaid the deed somewheres along the way. But the bill of sale copy's safe enough. I can close my eyes and see where it's at. That little piece of paper is your meal ticket, Richardson, the date on it is all you'll need to finish him off. Get him off your back for good."

They rode on in silence, crossing the Niotaze River and angling southwest toward the border of Indian territory to better avoid Sedan. Albert began waxing nostalgic, talking about his beloved Avvy. He didn't come right out and say it, but Horne got the distinct impression that he'd been sleeping with her for years. And that she truly loved him. Wanted him, needed him, willingly gave herself to him, but refused to marry. She'd made up her mind to that early on and stuck by her guns. He'd been patient, understanding, tolerant of her refusal to see the thing his way, but whenever the subject came up between them, it left him with a bitter taste and frustration boiling in his gut.

He had never been married. They had known one another for twenty years; four of those years she'd been married. She'd been faithful to her husband; Albert resigned himself to standing by, the trusted friend. He didn't say how they'd originally met, only that it started out a brother-sister arrangement. Her husband traveled a lot for the farm-equipment company that employed him. She was lonely; she needed a friend to talk to, preferably a man. After her husband died, Albert bided his time, allowing for a decent interval before launching his campaign to win her heart. He waited patiently nearly two years, and when he asked her for her hand and she turned him down, it devastated him.

But it did not discourage him.

"Every year 'round this time I'd propose. Every time I'd get the same answer. Let me tell you something, it's a helluva thing to have to live with."

"I can imagine."

"I don' think you can, unless you've been put through it. It's like a little kid walkin' by a candy store on his way to school every day. Lookin' in the window seein' a big box of chocolate-covered cherries, his favorite. They set his mouth waterin' somethin' fierce, and his heart achin' to taste just one. But he can't. He hasn' got the price. But that doesn' keep him from lookin' and yearnin', and there they sit day in day out with the window glass between him and them. And the achin' and wantin' just get worse and worse and worse."

"It's over now, Albert."

"Is it? That's how much you know."

They were passing through sandhills within sight of the border. Suddenly a bunch of riders appeared, coming from the north and slightly behind them. At full gallop, heading straight for them. They vanished behind a group of hills, then reappeared. Horne reckoned they were about half a mile away.

"Somebody in a hurry," commented Albert.

Closer and closer they drew. Horne and Albert had continued heading west. To their left more hills rose. Now the riders were directly behind them and coming fast. They began shooting.

"What the hell!" burst Albert. He swung about in his saddle, took one look, and widened his eyes. "Jesus Christ, it's Tewes!"

Before Horne could say one word, he spurred his horse savagely and took off. "Albert!"

Shots whistled by Horne. He ducked instinctively, hanging on to his hat with one hand and spurring his horse. Tewes and his deputies were closing the gap fast. Horne urged his horse to greater speed. Bullets whizzed past him on both sides. Hunched low in the saddle, he dug in his spurs. His horse flew forward, but Albert was moving much faster, stretching the distance separating them farther with every stride.

Disaster struck. Horne's horse's forehoof came down in a hole. The horse tilted to one side, stopped, and threw him. Over he sailed, landing viciously hard in the rain ditch. For a split-second he imagined every bone from his rear to his neck was broken. He rolled over. Tewes and his men came thundering by, still shooting at the fleeing

Albert. Their dust enveloped Horne, setting him coughing, grains seeding his eyes. He raised himself, bracing himself with one arm. The dust settled. Past Tewes and the others' backs he saw Albert take on in the back, throw his arms up, and topple from his saddle. On went his horse. He lay on his side still as death. Tewes and his men pulled up.

"You murdering sons of bitches," roared Horne. Ignoring the possibility of broken bones, he jumped to his feet and ran toward them. Miraculously, he's suffered no injury. He ran up to them raging.

They had dismounted and surrounded Albert. Tewes knelt and check his jugular. "Dead."

"You bastards! Did you have to kill him? Heartless, murdering—"

"Shut up," Tewes burst. "We didn't shoot him."

"We didn't," said one of the deputies. "We was just shooting to scare him into stopping. Shooting over his head, to the sides . . ."

"Then one of you is a rotten shot," snapped Horne.

"None of us hit him," insisted Tewes. "I gave strict orders. I just wanted to question him. We didn't shoot to kill. Sssssh . . ."

He held a finger against his lips. From behind the hills to their left came the sound of a horse setting off at a gallop. Tewes held his gesture for silence. The sound was already beginning to fade. Horse and rider emerged from cover, a quarter of a mile ahead. They watched the horse's dust slowly rise behind it, eventually obscuring sight of horse and rider. Horne didn't have to see who it was; he knew.

"There's your goddamn murderer," growled Tewes.

Horne's mind whirled. He swore viciously and kicked the ground, stubbing his toe, yelping in pain. Horse and rider were out of sight.

11

They took Albert Cutshaw's body back to Sedan. Horne paid an undertaker to prepare it for burial and forward it to Carl Junction. He made arrangements to return the horse he'd rented to Coffeyville and got out his own horse.

Sheriff Tewes did not understand why anyone would want to kill his prime suspect in the murder of Aveline Del Cassé. Horne enlightened him in detail. They stood in front of the sheriff's office.

"You saying you recognized this Kimbell at that distance?" Tewes asked.

"I didn't have to, it was him, all right. He had this scam of his all set up to euchre me out of the Cockeyed Coyote. The only possible stumbling block was Albert. He asked around, found out that Albert had left town, knew about Aveline, and came out here two days before I did, went straight to her house . . ."

"And killed her?"

"Albert sure didn't. He swore to me she was alive when he left there. My guess is Kimbell dropped by shortly after he left and questioned her about him. When she couldn't come up with the answers he wanted, he killed her. Maybe there was even another angle to it. Maybe she had her strongbox out, which gave him a second reason to do away with her, though he only needed one. He's your murderer, bet your life on it. After he left her, he probably looked around for Albert, couldn't find him, and gave it up. Went back to Muddy Springs. But when I took off from there, knowing I was going looking for Albert, he followed."

"You think he's gone back to Muddy Springs again?"

"Absolutely. With all the loose ends tied up, meaning Albert disposed of, he can now drop the hammer on me."

"We'll take a run over there and have a little talk."

"He'll be expecting you; he'll have six witnesses prepared to swear he never left town."

"Mmmmm. Offhand, I don't see any way of pinning either murder on him. No clues, no witnesses."

"What about me?"

"You just got through saying you didn't actually see it was him. Oh, you want it to be, you're convinced it was; that'd certainly solve your problem with him, but a judge and jury need proof."

"I know. Maybe I can get it for them."

"Do me a favor, keep an eye on him."

"I'll be on him like a hawk."

He wired Perry, telling him the bottom had dropped out of the thing; Kimbell had succeeded in knocking it out. He told him he would be back in Muddy Springs early the next evening.

It was about six when he rode into town: dusty, saddle-weary, discouraged. Typical T.G. Horne luck, he reflected sadly. He rode by the Coyote. Roy Pendleton's "Closed Until Further Notice" sign was tacked to the front. The swinging doors were covered by crossed boards. He went to the hotel, but Perry wasn't there. He rode out to Mary Alice Tubbs'.

He found Perry finishing supper. Paul Flanagan was also Mary Alice's guest. All three greeted him effusively, all three with pity in their eyes. Mary Alice fed him vegetable soup and homemade wheat bread with freshly churned butter. He told them everything that had happened. Flanagan listened with his eyes on the floor. He did not look up until Horne had finished.

"Cutshaw never said where he had the bill of sale?"

"He refused to tell me. I can't blame him, it's my ace

and he put a price on it. He couldn't take chances. If you think about it, he didn't know me from Adam."

"I guess that's that," interposed Perry. "Kimbell wins, you lose."

"You're not giving up," burst Mary Alice.

"We don't have much left to continue fighting with," said Flanagan wearily.

"Is Kimbell back?" Horne asked Perry.

"Early this morning. He's been throwing money around like a drunken sailor all day."

"Aveline Del Cassé's money, the thieving bastard. Excuse me, Mary Alice. How are Roy and Elliott and the girls?"

"Hanging on, waiting, still drawing their pay as per your instructions. Which reminds me, your well-developed friend Miss Hopwell. . ."

"What about her?"

"You tell me. I was standing in front of the Coyote yesterday morning, passing the time of day with her when Kimbell walked by. Hang on to your chair; they recognized each other."

"Star and Kimbell?"

Perry nodded. "Didn't greet each other, not a word passed between them, but you could tell. The look on his face, on hers. He never broke stride, just sashayed on by. You should have seen her expression. She suddenly looked like somebody was holding a gun at her back."

"Did you ask her about him?"

"Not me. You're the one who should ask her. I wasn't about to shove my oar in. I just thought you ought to know."

"Interesting. You know something, I remember her telling me she worked all over Nevada before she came back here. He was out there."

"They know each other," Perry said. "Bet on it. I suggest you go over to her place and have a little chat. Maybe she can tell you something helpful about the dog in the manger."

"I can't imagine what," said Flanagan. "The whole thing hinges on the documents, and he's got 'em. They predate

yours, rendering yours worthless. Unquestionably, with
Cutshaw removed from the picture. Damnation! Why did
the damned fool have to go and get himself shot."

"I can assure you," murmured Horne, "it wasn't inten-
tional on his part."

Flanagan rose from his chair. "Supper was delicious,
Mary Alice. I appreciate a home-cooked meal more than
most, and I thank you for inviting me. I have to go. I have
to get in touch with Judge Coombes up in Wellington."
He glanced at Horne. "I have to play square with him;
he's got to know about this."

"So soon?" Horne asked. "Can't you hold off a day or
so?"

"Can't you?" Perry asked.

"I don't see what for. Maybe till tomorrow afternoon. I
can't pussyfoot with him; he trusts me. If he thought I was
trying to pull a fast one, he'd flay me alive. Good night,
all."

It was dark by the time Horne got to Star Hopwell's
boardinghouse. She answered his knock. Recognizing him,
she assumed a guilty expression. he couldn't imagine why
she should react so upon seeing him, but didn't give her a
chance to explain, if she intended to. In he walked without being invited, bolted the door, and before she could
say one word other than her greeting, launched his narra-
tive. He told her everything from the time he left town to
when he came back an hour before. Everything, except
his introduction to Joan C. Calhoun. But then that had no
bearing on the issue at hand.

"You do know Kimbell, right?"

"Don't look at me like that, T.G., Ah'm not gonna deny
it. Ah met him when ah was workin' in Silvermine, a
saloon in Tonkin. We had a thing goin' for a while, but it
was mostly him. Ah was afraid o' him, still am. He can be
a rough customer. I wanted out, but he wouldn' heah o' it.
Ah nearly died on the spot when he walked by me and
Mr. Marblehall the othah mawnin'."

"He went to prison for killing somebody out there."

'Jeff Kelleher. He liked me; he was a nice fella. Ah liked

him, only Ah was scared to break up with Addison. He can be downright vicious. They got into a fight ovah me, Jeff about killed him. Latah that night Addison hid in a alley, ambushed him walkin' by in the dahk, jumped him, killed him. Broke his neck."

"He what?"

"Broke his neck. Addison's got real strong ahms. He stands 'hind youh, slips his fohahm under youh chin, sets his othah elbow on your shouldah, clamps the inside o' his right foham undah his left hand, sets his right hand 'gainst the back o' youh haid, and pushes fohwahd. Snappo! He showed me a couple times, huht me, too. That man scared the livin' daylights outta me."

"He killed Aveline Del Cassé by breaking her neck."

"Theah's somethin' I gotta tell youh. I mean he terrifies me. He . . . Don' go gettin' mad, T.G., I couldn' help myself. He . . . well, he slept heah last night. Ah had to do it, he made me."

"Something else I owe the son of a bitch for!"

"His claim to the Coyote, it's phony. Knowin' him it just has to be."

"I know, only there doesn't seem to be any way of proving it is."

"Maybe they is, maybe not. He slept heah last night; he was drunk. Not roarin' drunk just, youh know, tipsy. When he drinks, he talks in his sleep." Horne perked up. "He said a couple things, a fella's name. Talked about Cahson City, the pen'tentiary, Ah mean. Fella who was in the same cell with him. He was a ahtist like the ones who draw the papah money."

"Engraver."

"He said ahtist. Said he was a genyus. Theah wasn' nothin' he couldn' copy. Draw anythin'. Make it look like the real thing so even a expeht couldn' tell. Oh, he didn't say those wuhds, but that was the gist o' it, youh know?"

"Draw anything. From memory. Kimbell's. A deed, a bill of sale."

"He lay theah mumblin'. It come out one wuhd at a time, the way folks talk in theah sleep, youh know. He kep' sayin' dice, heaht. Does that make sense?"

"Dice, heart . . ."

"Like roll the dice, bless youh heaht."

"Dice, heart, dice, heart, diceheart. Dysart. That's a name; German, I think."

"He mumbled it three or fouh times: Cahson City, Dysaht, ahtist, terrific, genyus, copyin', pitchahs, money, han'writin', anythin' . . ."

"Fabulous! Tremendous! Listen to me, they were cellmates, both released at or close to the same time. He made a deal with Dysart to whip up those phony papers and euchre me out of the Coyote."

"But he was cleah out to Nevada; how would he know youh'd taken ovah from Cutshaw?"

"He didn't at first. But found out somehow. Then went to Dysart and put him to work. I wonder where Dysart is now?"

"He didn' mumble that; everythin' he said was like his mind was back in prison."

"Kimbell knows where he is! I can't make him tell me, but there has to be some way I can find out." He got up.

"Youh not goin' so soon?"

"I'll be back. I have to see Flanagan. This is dynamite!"

"Youh bettah not come back tonight, T.G., Addison'll be comin'. If theah's any trouble, if theahs a ruckus, that ol' bat of a lan'lady'll throw me out. We're not s'posed to let men in the room. But he'll sure be comin' 'round."

"Will you be all right?"

"Sure. He won' cripple me or nothin' like that. He'll jus' wanna have his way with me. Ah let him." she shuddered. " 'Fraid not to, he scares me so. He's a bastahd. Ah was crazy to evah hook up with him in the fuhst place."

Horne drew his Sharps .22 from its holster at the small of his back.

"Stick this under your pillow just in case."

"Oh, no no, Ah'm scared to death o' guns. Ah nevah fiahed one in mah life. Nevah would dare. Ah'd prob'ly shoot mahself if Ah tried."

He produced his dagger-mounted knuckle-duster.

She waved it away. "Ah'll be okay, don' youh worry

none. They's only one thing he evah wants from me, and ah can't believe he'd kill the goose that lays . . ."

"The golden egg."

"Ah don' lay eggs, mistuh."

She laughed and waved him away. He wasn't three steps from her door outside when around the corner at the end of the hall came the vision of loveliness he'd encountered at the back door on his previous visit. He tipped his hat. She intensified the ugliness ravaging her face and nodded curtly.

Across the street from the boardinghouse Addison Kimbell stood in the shadows in an alley. He lit a cigarette and drew deeply. He had seen Horne enter the house, walking down the side to the rear stairs. Now he watched him emerge from the darkness, watched him cross to the front walk, glowing a pale yellow from the light of the porch lamp. He came down the walk, turned left at the end, and walked off.

As Horne turned at the end of the approach walk, a woman came into sight from the opposite direction. She was tall, willowy, but shapeless; flat as his hand out front, Kimbell mused. He watched her cross the front of the house, round the corner, and vanish into the darkness on her way to the rear stairs. He followed her with squinting eyes every step until she disappeared, but did not recognize her. He'd never seen her before. Where, he wondered, was she heading? Did she live there? Probably. It was a little late in the evening to be visiting.

Kimbell smoked, finished his cigarette, and flicked away the butt. Then he crossed the street and followed the woman's route. He ascended the back stairs. The door was unlocked. In he went, rounding the corner, moving down the narrow hallway to Star's door.

When she opened in response to his knock, she tried very hard to keep her face from falling to show her disappointment. But did not altogether succeed. He came in frowning.

"Whatsa mattah, Addison?" she asked worriedly.

"Should something be the matter? Have you done something to make me angry? You wouldn't do that, would you, dear heart?" He reached behind him and slid the bolt. "What are you looking so worried about?"

"Nothin'."

"Nothing. You sure? Aren't you going to ask me to sit down?" She gestured to the chair; he took it. She backed away, standing near the head of the bed, her back close to the wall. "Aren't you going to sit down?" She sat on the bed, fussing aimlessly with the sheet, her eyes downcast, as if unable to meet his. "What are you looking so for? What's the matter? Tell me."

"Nothin', Ah'm fine."

"I see you had a visitor."

"Me? Ah didn't neithah."

"Mr. Richardson, Horne, whatever he's calling himself these days."

"Oh him . . ."

"Him."

"Ah fohgot, he stopped by a few seconds."

"What for?"

"Just to, youh know, say hello. He's been outta town; just got back tonight."

"You and he have a nice long talk? What about?"

"Nothin', hones'!"

"Why the guilty look? Have you been telling tales out of school? What did you talk about? Tell me. What did you tell him? About us back in Tonkin? The old days? That couldn't have been very interesting to him. Boyfriend hearing about his girl's old beaus has to be pretty dull stuff."

"He's not mah boyfriend."

"That's not what I hear. I hear he's smitten with you. You like him? You must, you wouldn't be letting him in your room this time of night. Come on, tell me what you talked about. What you told him. About us. About me."

"Nothin', I keep tellin' youh! Why don'cha believe me, Chrissakes!"

"Tut tut tut tut, foul language. Come here."

She stood up and started to remove her kimono. "I didn't say take your clothes off, I said come here." She edged toward him, her eyes saucering, swimming with fear. Her lips quivered, she couldn't keep her hands still. She began to bite her lower lip.

"What are you so nervous about? Come here, I said, closer."

She stood before him, six inches separating them. He got up. He towered over her. He took her by the throat. The last of her color drained from her cheeks. She tried to cry out, but he tightened his grip, cutting the sound off sharply.

"Don't . . . don't make a sound. I won't hurt you. Would I hurt you, dear heart? Would I?"

She lowered her eyes and struggled to keep from trembling.

"Would I? Answer me!"

"Nnnnno."

He slapped her hard, sending her head swerving savagely right, so sharply the pain in her neck hurt as much as the slap.

"That didn't hurt, did it? Not really." Again he set his hands to her throat. He did not tighten, but held it securely, so that she could not have freed herself if she tried. She didn't dare.

"For the last time, dear heart, what did you tell him about me?"

It was getting on to nine o'clock. Horne hurried his step. There was a good chance Paul Flanagan had gone back to his office after leaving Mary Alice Tubbs' house. He worked most evenings, often as late as midnight; work was about all he had to fill his hours, day and night.

He had to tell somebody what he'd found out! Dysart. It was the first break in the storm clouds. Oh, catching up with Cutshaw was the very first, but when he dropped from his horse with Kimbell's bullet in him, the clouds sealed right back up again.

Dysart. Dysart. If only he had a location for him. If only he had his first name. There had to be some way to establish his present whereabouts. God bless Star! Bless her loyalty, her courage; unlike most of her free-living sisters, she had substance to her, principles, values: a sense of justice, of right and wrong.

And she loved him, would do anything for him. Even risk her life. Which, confiding in him, was exactly what she was doing. He owed her his protection. He had come to care more deeply for her than he'd ever thought possible. Separated from her these couple days he'd often thought about her and had missed her. Wouldn't it be wonderful if everything worked out his way, Kimbell was permanently blocked from interfering, gave up, and left town. Things would get back to normal, business would resume booming, he and Star would be together every day, every night. . .

Flanagan's second-floor office was in darkness when he approached the building. He'd evidently left Mary Alice's and gone home to bed. The good news would have to keep until morning. He turned around, walked the four blocks to the hotel, and went to bed.

Paul Xavier Flanagan had been cold-sober when he said good-night to them and left Mary Alice's. But when Horne walked in on him the next morning, he found him fire-eyed and suffering a splitting headache, popping Schenck's pills into his mouth and wincing accompaniment to the shooting pains attacking the contents of his skull at five-second intervals.

"You look great," said Horne, "bright-eyed, chipper, sharp as a tack, ready to take on the world."

"I stayed up a little late. You look a lot happier than you did last night. What's going on?"

"I think I've found the chink in Kimbell's armor."

He started to recount his conversation with Star. He didn't get far. A knock rattled the door. Flanagan held up a visibly trembling hand.

"Come in."

It was Marshal Bronkowski. Ignoring Flanagan, he fastened a frown on Horne. "I figured I'd find you here when you weren't in your hotel room." He took a step backward and whipped out his gun. "Get your hands up. Paul, take off his gun belt. Pat him down for other weapons. Don't overlook his boot pistol."

"What the hell is this?" growled Horne.

Flanagan was staring dumbfounded. "Marshal . . ."

"Do as I say, Paul" Flanagan shrugged, mystified, and went about his task. "You're under arrest, Mr. Gambling Man. For murder."

"You're crazy!"

"The murder of one Star Hopwell, a woman employed by you and residing at number twelve East Street. Found dead in her room this morning."

"Oh, my God . . ."

"By her landlady."

"I didn't do it!"

"Shut up, T.G." snapped Flanagan. "You don't have to say one word."

"Lying on the floor . . ." Bronkowski went on.

"Her neck broken."

"How'd you know that if you didn't do it?"

"Kimbell did it. That's how he kills, his trademark. He did it, I tell you!"

"Do as he says, son, clam up. You might say something to make things even worse for you."

"I didn't kill her!"

"That's not for me to decide. Come along quietly, please? Don't make me get rough."

"Go with him T.G. Cooperate, we'll straighten this out."

"Oh, for Chrissakes . . ."

"His anger had set his stomach in turmoil; it was so ridiculous, so stupid, so outrageously unfair.

"We got an eyewitness saw you leave her room," Bronkowski went on. "Doc Pulsifer examined the body, and he figures the time of death to be just about the time the witness saw you leaving there. Let's go."

Wary-eyeing him as he would an ax murderer, Bronkowski marched him down the stairs at gunpoint, but when they got outside, he holstered his weapon. A woman came running up. Horne recognized her as the one he'd passed in the hallway upon leaving Star's room. The one he'd mistaken for Star in the darkness of the back-door landing on his first visit.

"That's him, Marshal! I saw him coming out her door bold as brass. Mr. Innocence, and all the time with her blood on his hands. Murderer! Monster!"

Her shrill voice was attracting the attention of passersby. People on both sides of them stopped and stared. Across the street a young woman monitoring a group of little girls gawked at him. A few of the children were pointing. All eyes fastened on him as his accuser continued berating him; embarrassment consumed him. He wanted to shrivel up and sink between the sidewalk slats at his feet.

"Take it easy, Miss Van Atta," growled the marshal. "What are you doing here anyway? I got your statement, you signed it; go about your business!"

"You ought to be stoned to death by every man, woman, and child in town. Attacking a poor, defenseless woman! Raping and killing! You brute! Disgusting animal!"

People nearby watching her carry on began clucking disapproval, shaking their heads at him. One man glared and shook his fist. Miss Van Atta took a step toward him, raising her parasol menacingly.

Bronkowski barred her way and pushed her back with his forearm. "I said get out of here!"

She scowled pitchforks, turned, and hurried off, talking to herself, seething.

Bronkowski started them off in the opposite direction, holding Horne by the upper arm. "Go about your business, folks."

Horne walked through a gauntlet of stares and hushed comments. His cheeks tingled; he kept his eyes on the sidewalk. They got to the corner and turned it, escaping the rubberneckers. Out of sight of them he could still hear their buzzing.

"Sorry about that," said the marshal. "You've got to understand, I'm only doing my duty. If you didn't do it, if you can prove your innocence, you've got nothing to worry about."

"I'll get that son of a bitch Kimbell!"

"Now, now . . ."

"I'll kill him! So help me God I will!"

"Simmer down; accusing somebody else is no way to go about defending yourself."

"Do me a small favor, Marshal."

"If I can, if I don't have to break the law."

"You won't."

"What is it?"

"Just shut up."

12

Two of the most miserable days of his lifetime passed at a slug's gait for Horne. He sat in his cell thinking, mired in frustration, feeling sorry for himself, reviling the fates, staring into space. His situation physically sickened him. To add to his wretchedness, he learned that the Cockeyed Coyote had reopened under new management. Kimbell's grand opening featured drinks on the house for the first hundred patrons through the door. And rumor had it that he planned to do away with the gambling casino and convert it into a whorehouse.

Flanagan and Perry visited Horne regularly. Mary Alice came, as did Roy and Elliott, Francine-Mae and Eula-Mae. All were sympathetic and optimistic, but his own flourishing pessimism more than offset their combined well-intended encouragement.

Perry showed up middle of the afternoon of his third day behind bars.

"Where the hell have you been?" snapped Horne.

"Don't start, T.G.; out running my aching legs off on your behalf, thank you, you're welcome. With Paul Flanagan all morning, helping him prepare your defense."

"What defense? I don't have any. I'm as good as hanged. What the hell are they waiting for?"

"Thatta boy, think positive. This Dysart, Kimbell's cellmate in prison . . ."

"If we could only track that son of a bitch down."

"Why bother? I don't see as he can do anything for you

in this. Do yourself a favor, stop carrying on like a martyr going to the stake. You're not guilty—ergo, you're not going to hang."

"I am!"

"Will you two quiet down in there, please?" asked Bronkowski from out front.

"Guess what," said Perry, "We've found Emil."

"Who?"

Emil Dysart."

Horne started and scowled fiercely. "Why didn't you say so in the first place? How?"

"Paul wired the warden at the penitentiary. This came back half an hour ago." He unfolded a telegram. Horne read:

> DYSART WOULD BE EMIL DYSART
> STOP ADDRESS AT TIME OF ARREST
> FORGERY RENO STOP PRIOR TO RENO
> WELLINGTON KANSAS
>   D. HORNBECK
>   WARDEN
>   CARSON CITY PENITENTIARY

"Oh, boy . . ."

"I thought that might pick you up a smidgen. Though, as I said before, I can't see what good it'll do us."

"Don't you understand? Dysart phonied Kimbell's deed and bill of sale for him, even to forging the notary stamps. The man does beautiful work."

"Don't *you* understand . . ."

"What?"

"You think Dysart will admit it? He'd be crazy to. He's an ex-con; he opens his mouth and he'll go right back inside. Chinese water torture won't get it out of him. You might just as well ask him to put a gun to his head."

"I know that, but the fact remains he did it. Kimbell paid him and he delivered. Kimbell knows it, Dysart knows it, it's a reality. There's got to be some way on God's green earth to prove it."

"If you can think of one, more power to you. I've racked

my feeble brain and it beats me. Let's put that aside for the moment. That's the good news."

"What's the bad?"

"You go on trial tomorrow morning."

"Tomor—"

"The wheels of injustice grind rapidly it seems. At least in Kansas."

"It's insane. I didn't touch her; I didn't! Believe it or not, I was falling in love with her. When I was away, she was constantly on my mind. I wouldn't dream of harming her."

"I'm sure. Only how can we prove you didn't?"

"I thought it was the other way around; whatever happened to you're innocent until you're proven guilty?"

"In this case, alas, that evidently constitutes a minor technical point. Let's face it, the Van Atta woman's sworn statement is damaging as hell. We've got to find some way to discredit it. Let's go over the thing one more time."

"We've been over it twenty times. And I've been over it twenty more with Paul. I haven't forgotten anything, I can't add anything." He sighed heavily. "Poor Star, poor little girl. Did I tell you I tried to give her my derringer to protect herself? She refused it. Damn, if she'd only taken it. She'd be alive, he'd be dead, the Coyote would be mine . . ."

"He'd be dead and she'd probably be sitting here instead of you."

A shadow fell between them. It was Bronkowski. His face wore a sheepish expression. His tone sounded almost apologetic.

"Excuse me, boys, I just want to say I'm damned sorry about this mess. Honestly. If it'll help any, I personally don't believe you did it. You're not the type goes around strangling women. Let me ask you something, do you recall seeing anybody besides miss Van Atta when you left the room? Inside the house, out back, out front, anywhere close by?"

"I've cudgeled my brain over that one. I don't remember a soul. Not even in the street until I got to the corner.

And anybody who saw me there wouldn't know where I was coming from."

"Too bad."

"Let me ask you something, Marshal. How can you charge me with murder in the first degree? Isn't that premeditated murder?"

"It is," said Bronkowski, "but that's how this figures. I have to go by the circumstances. It happened in her home, you were visiting. If it was the other way around, if she'd come to see you, bringing herself within your reach, so to speak, of her own . . ."

"Volition," interposed Perry.

"Right. Then it wouldn't be premeditated, unless the prosecution could prove you lured her there, tricked her into walking into your trap. That's the way it works, at least in this state." Bronkowski shook his head. "I sure do wish somebody else saw you that night."

"So do I, Marshal. So do I."

13

The courtroom was jammed. Attorney Felix D. F. Magnusson, prosecuting for the state, rose six-feet-eight from his shiny leather heels. He was handsome, a consummate actor, learned, shrewd, and extraordinarily quick on his feet, according to Paul Flanagan. In every respect a worthy opponent to the little man. Standing side by side before Judge Coombes, their backs to the principals and spectators, they looked like father and small son, although bald pates like Flanagan's were seldom seen on seven-year-olds.

Magnusson asked Horne to take the stand. He lost no time in bringing his heaviest artillery to bear.

"Mr. Horne," Mr. Richardson . . . which do you prefer to be called?"

"Horne," mumbled Horne.

"Why the alias? People with two names generally have something to hide. Do you have something to hide, Mr. Horne?"

"Objection," boomed Flanagan. "The defendant is not on trial for what he calls himself. That's his business; it doesn't concern us."

"Sustained," murmured Judge Coombes. "Let's get on with it, Felix."

His honor was more severe-looking than Horne would have wished. He hadn't expected a happy-go-lucky, light-hearted character at the business end of the gavel, but would have appreciated someone with a little warmth in their face. Coombes was so serious as to be downright intimidating, and T.G. wondered if he was capable of smiling.

Magnusson paused in his pacing to impale Horne to the back of his chair with a suspicious eye. "Mr. Horne, have you ever been arrested before?"

"I—"

"A simple yes or no will suffice."

"Yes."

"Charged with murder?"

Horne's eyes flew to Flanagan and Perry sitting beside him. He stirred uneasily in the witness chair.

"I didn't hear you, Mr. Horne."

"Yes."

A rumble ran through the spectators. Judge Coombes rapped his gavel. Magnusson leered.

"I was found innocent in both cases."

"I didn't ask you that," said Magnusson in a hurt tone. "Your honor, would you kindly instruct the defendant to confine himself to answering my questions?"

"Mr. Horne . . ." began Coombes.

"Okay, Your Honor."

Magnusson referred to a paper affixed to his clipboard. "Isn't it a fact that you were arrested and charged with murdering one Louis DeBlois in Juneau, Alaska, last year?"

"Yes, but—"

"And two years previous to that arrested and charged with the murder of one Lincoln Hogandyke in Payton, New Mexico. The jury found you guilty, you were sentenced to hang."

"The sentence was overturned."

"If Your Honor please . . ."

"Mr. Horne."

"You're a professional gambler, isn't that so? That's your business, your way of earning your living. How long have you been so engaged?"

"About fourteen years."

"About fourteen years. Since you were a boy. A wandering parasite living off the unwary and the ignorant by cheating at cards. You do cheat, do you not?"

"I—"

"I'll accept that as an affirmative answer."

"I object," boomed Flanagan. "This is out-and-out character assassination!"

"Your Honor, I'm only painting the defendant's character to establish what stripe of man we have here."

"Overruled. Proceed."

"Mr. Horne, you're expert at manipulating cards, dice, gambling devices. Were you or were you not run out of Hooksville recently? Tarred and feathered, run out of town on a rail?" He leaned close, his eyes drilling, tone venomous; his face looked as if he'd bitten into something sour. "Caught redhanded cheating at poker."

"Not true!"

"Then why were you run out of town?"

"I—"

"Oh, my error. I beg your pardon. My apologies, Mr. Horne, it was your friend and companion Mr. Youngquist who was doing the cheating. And the two of you were tarred and feathered. In sum, sir, you yourself not only cheat, but you habitually consort with others guilty of the same immorality, the same crime. Your Honor, gentlemen of the jury, ladies and gentlemen, I ask you to look closely at this man. This parasite, this pariah. Decent, honest people shun men of his ilk; he connives and consorts with the dregs of society. Only they will tolerate his presence. Only they are his friends and companions.

"He's the first one on the scene when gold is discovered. The first when cattle money comes to town. No one—man, woman or child—is safe from his depredations. He will cheat the parson, the teacher, the honest tradesman, the pillar of society, anyone and everyone he can lure into his net. He cheats; he swindles, dupes, deceives, and defrauds without a twinge of conscience. He lives on the edge of the law, in trouble and wriggling out of it time and again. And whither he goest, thither and yon, he leaves a trail of broken lives, ruined lives, innocent wives and babes wantonly deprived of the family wage earner's money. These vipers, the professional gamblers in our midst, are responsible for more suicides than any other criminal group infecting society.

"This particular professional gambler has gone even further. Has brutally murdered an innocent and defenseless woman."

Flanagan shot to his feet. "Objection! Objection! Objection! Defendant is accused, Your Honor, learned counsel has produced no proof of guilt."

Magnusson held up a paper. "Proof. Your Honor, gentlemen of the jury, I have here the sworn statement of Miss Henrietta Van Atta, a communicant of the First Baptist Church and leader of the choir, a boarder in the same house where the victim lived. With Your Honor's permission I should like to read a few lines."

"Proceed."

"He—meaning the defendant—came out of her room, closing the door behind him. He walked right by me. When I got to my room two doors down from the victim's, I turned up my lamp and looked at my watch. It was twenty-five minutes to ten.

"Your Honor, let the record show that Dr. Omar Pulsifer examined the victim's remains shortly after the body was discovered the next morning. Dr. Pulsifer set the time of death as between a quarter past nine and a quarter to ten the previous night. I have Dr. Pulsifer's sworn statement to that affect."

Henrietta Van Atta's statement alone made his case to Magnusson's satisfaction. He announced that he was through questioning Horne and turned him over to Paul Flanagan. Nothing in the testimony he elicited from Horne could undo the damage inflicted by the Van Atta woman's statement. Flanagan's questions and Horne's responses speedily became an exercise in futility. Groping for something, anything that might cast even the suggestion of doubt on the woman's indictment, Flanagan began to flounder. Horne's heart sank even lower as he sensed it, and he was actually relieved when Flanagan finally gave it up.

"Do either of you want to call Miss Van Atta to the witness stand?" asked Judge Coombes.

"Not necessary, Your Honor," sang Magnusson.

"No, Your Honor," said Flanagan.

"Any other witnesses?"

There were none. Judge Coombes requested Magnusson's closing statement. In a brief, grandiloquent if somewhat boring speech, Magnusson declared:

"I see no need to take up the court's valuable time by repeating what has already been stated. The facts speak eloquently for themselves. I leave it to my worthy opponent to make his last ditch attempt to refute them."

Flanagan too declined to close. Horne couldn't blame him. What could he say to change anything? Nothing he could think of. Coombes rapped his gavel.

"Gentlemen of the jury, you've heard the testimony in this case. It is now for you to decide the guilt or innocence of the defendant. You may consult among yourselves."

"Your Honor! Your Honor! Your Honor!"

Horne's, Perry's, and every other head save the judge's turned at the loud, shrill voice coming from the rear. Horne recognized Ora-Mae Strickland, the willowy brunette with the chest as full and rounded as an ironing board. Overdressed from feathered hat to sequined shoes, waving her parasol, she came surging up the aisle.

"Hold everything!"

"Who are you? What is the meaning of this? How dare you interrupt—" rasped a suddenly red-faced Coombes.

"Somebody's got to before you railroad this poor fellow into the grave. He no more murdered Star Hopwell than you did. I know, and I can prove it. You gonna hear me out or aren't cha?"

"Ahem, approach the bench."

Ora-Mae swept between Magnusson's table and Flanagan's up to the bench. The judge rose from his seat and leaned over to converse with her. They talked in whispers. Everyone close leaned forward to hear what was being said, but no one could. Everyone waited. Horne glanced at Magnusson. He looked totally confused, as did Flanagan. Judge Coombes straightened.

"Extraordinary. Gentlemen of the jury, you are hereby instructed to cease your deliberations."

"We've already 'rived at a verdict, Your Honor," piped the foreman.

"Keep it to yourselves." Down came the gavel loudly. "There will be a thirty-minute recess. Mr. Magnusson, Mr. Flanagan, Mr. Horne, Miss . . ."

"Ora-Mae Strickland, I tol' ja."

"The four of you will join me in my chambers."

Confusion erupted. Again Coombes rapped his gavel.

"What the hell . . ." murmured Flanagan mystified.

Both attorneys, Horne and Ora-Mae sat before the judge in his chambers.

"Speak up, Miss . . ."

"Strickland."

"Tell them what you told me."

"Your Honor," protested Magnusson, "this woman hasn't even been sworn. If she's a witness—"

"Just relax, Felix. This isn't court. Miss . . ."

"Okay. Like I tol' ja, he no more murdered Star than you did. I oughta know, I saw him leaving the house. I was coming up the sidewalk from the other direction. He turned left when he got to the sidewalk and put his back to me so's he couldn't see me. But I saw you, T.G., big as life. I nearly called to you, but you looked like you were in a hurry. Your Honor, I worked for him, T.G.; tell him, T.G. Worked with Star, the victim, and I'm telling you I saw her and spoke to her *after* he left her. She was alive, she was just fine. My room was four doors down from hers. I stopped by her door not two minutes after he left. Like I tol' ja, Judge, she'd borrowed a pair of green satin pumps from me and I wanted 'em back on account I was leaving town early the next morning."

"Your Honor—" began Magnusson.

"Shhh, go on, Miss . . ."

"Ora-Mae Strickland. Can' cha remember? Anyway, I heard that snake Kimbell who stole the Coyote from T.G. was planning to turn it into a cathouse, and I was damned if I'd go back to lyin' on my back for the likes of him."

"We can skip over that," said Coombes, running his finger inside his collar.

"Not on your tintype, so I decided to leave town. Go home to Wichita and find a job waitressing, tending bar, anything except whoring."

"Ahem, yes," murmured the judge.

"I bought my train ticket. I was leaving on the eight-thirty A.M. I stopped by Star's room on my way out. I knocked and knocked, but of course there was no answer, her laying inside dead and all. I left, left town. Yesterday I picked up the newspaper and there big as a buffalo was all this. I come back fast as I could, T.G."

"Fast enough, thank the Lord," said Horne.

"Miss Strickland," interposed Magnusson, "are you aware that we have a signed statement from another boarder, a Miss Henrietta Van Atta. She swears—"

"I know her. God almighty, what a face! Like it was set on by the dogs and healed. And the biggest mouth in Christendom."

"She swears she saw Mr. Horne leaving Miss Hopwell's room."

"So what? Does that prove he killed her? How could that be? I just got through telling you I saw him *outside* the house, then went in myself, straight to her room. And she was okay."

"Are you prepared to swear to that?" Coombes asked.

"Didn't I already tell you I would? Get a bible, get a bible!"

"Felix?"

Magnusson reflected a moment, chewing his lower lip, from the expression on his face already mentally capitulating.

"Felix?"

"I'm sold. The sovereign State of Kansas herewith drops all charges. You win, Paul."

14

Horne insisted on buying Ora-Mae dinner, buying her clothes, buying her something to show his gratitude. She refused to accept a thing. He had to settle for reimbursing her for her train fare. Twenty minutes after he got his freedom back he helped her board the train to Wichita. Making sure he got her address before she left.

"You'll be hearing from me, Ora-Mae. Kimbell may think he's won the ball game, but it's not over yet. I've still got one more at bat. Don't be surprised if we're back in business just like before in a week or so."

He kissed her gratefully good-bye and waved her away as the train pulled out.

"What did you tell her that for?" asked Perry and Flanagan simultaneously.

"Because I believe it. The tide has turned, gentlemen; Kimbell doesn't know it yet, but he's finished. And when I get him out of the Coyote, I'm going after him for what he did to that little girl. To Albert Cutshaw, Aveline. He's going to hang, my friends, I promise you. Now, if you'll both excuse me, I think I'll go have a friendly word with him."

"Wait a minute. Are you crazy?"

"What's crazy about talking to him? I said friendly word, didn't I? Trust me. Want to come along? I'm buying. I feel like celebrating."

Both declined and went off together.

Kimbell was behind the bar helping Elliott when Horne

walked in. The place was fairly crowded, unusual for the time of day, not yet three in the afternoon. Horne felt a small tug of envy watching money being put into the new cash register.

"Richardson! Alistair!" boomed Kimbell expansively. "Or do you prefer T.G.?"

"Whatever."

"Congratulations on getting off. I have to tell you I was worried. Things looked pretty dark there for a while. Your alibi showed up in the nick of time. What'll it be?"

"A glass of DeLoche's brandy would hit the spot."

Kimbell served him. Horne reached for his money. Kimbell gestured him not to bother. "It's on the house."

It should be, thought Horne bleakly. It's my liquor.

Kimbell laid a friendly hand on his shoulder. "I always admire a good loser."

"Me, too." Horne raised his glass in a toast, "Here's to you."

The play on words went right by Kimbell. He grinned. Horne grinned back and hated him so tenaciously, so profoundly, that he had to consciously steel himself to keep from flinging the brandy in his face and lunging for his throat. His liquor, his bar, customers, casino, his girl . . . He glanced past Kimbell and to the right. His framed deed, which had been hanging alongside the mirror, was no longer there.

"My deed," he said, pointing to the empty spot.

"I've got it. I put it in the safe." Kimbell got it out and handed it to him in its frame. "I took good care of it. I figured you'd be coming around for it. Souvenir, right?"

"Of happier, more prosperous days, yes." Again Horne toasted him. "To your health, Addison." May it fail you completely, he thought.

He emptied his glass, waved graciously, and left.

He walked over to the marshal's office and reclaimed his weapons. Darryl, another deputy, and Bronkowski congratulated him. They shook his hand.

"I knew you didn't do it," said the marshal.

"You did, I didn't."

"Where to now?"

"Oh, I'm not leaving town yet—that is, not for good."

"You going to try to get back the Coyote?"

"Wish me luck."

"I do. Just don't do anything foolish."

Twenty-three miles to Wellington. On the way he stopped off at Mary Alice's. At sight of him she threw her arms around him gleefully.

"I was there; I couldn't take that wise-aleck lawyer villifying you; I walked out before she showed up. My neighbor across the way came over and told me. Glory be and thanks to the good Lord; I hate to say it, but when I walked out of there, I thought the next time I see him—"

"He'll be dancing at the end of a rope. For a while there I was sure of it."

"How's about a cup of tea?"

"A quick one. I'm on my way to Wellington."

"What for?"

She put the pot on; they sat in the kitchen. He told her about Emil Dysart, his association with Kimbell and the service he'd performed for him.

"How can you be sure this Dysart came back to Wellington?"

"It seems logical. He had to be close by for Kimbell to be able to get together with him. In the area. Frankly, I'll be surprised if I don't find him there."

"You want the Coyote back so bad you can taste it."

"I want Kimbell a lot more. He's killed four people, Mary Alice, and that's just counting the ones I know about. It could be twenty-four. He killed Star; that alone is more than enough for me."

"So you're buckling on the terrible swift sword of vengeance. Setting yourself up as judge and jury."

"You don't approve?"

"Oh, I approve. Heartily. In certain circumstances a body has to act on his own: when nobody else, including the law, seems to be interested."

"He's gotten away with it so far. What's to stop him from killing and killing again?"

"You. You remind me of my Ephraim. When he pinned

on his U.S. marshal's badge, he got that same look in his eye. Of course he didn't go after some rascal who'd murdered his best girl." She laughed. "He better not have had a best girl. But hallelujah, what a bulldog! For peanuts. Six cents a mile and two dollars per arrest; nothing if you brought back a corpse. He and one of his friends were sent out after a wanted who'd robbed a couple of Wells Fargo depots and the bank in Argonia. Back then outlaws used to run down over the border into Indian territory to get away from the law. They were safe down there among their own kind and the redskins. Ephraim and his partner chased this one down into the Panhandle, No-Man's-Land.

"They were gone a week. I worried to death. The nights especially were hell on earth." She finished her tea and bit off a chaw. "I'd finish the chores, eat supper here in the kitchen, go into the parlor, chew some, sew some, read a little, and go to bed and lie there wondering what was happening. Was he alive or dead? Was he hurt, lying bleeding to death in a ditch? And not a word coming up from there. No wires, no way of sending a letter. A week, two weeks. By the end of the third week I was so skittish I was ready to crawl out of my skin and hang it on the wall. I was in bed one night—it was early winter, the wind bullying about the eaves—I heard horses, then thumping at the door. When I opened it, in he fell. His arm was in a rag of a sling. He had a bullet in his shoulder and one inside his right thigh. He was in a bad way, delirious, babbling. I dragged him across the floor to here, got him up onto the table, and went to work."

She raised her hand as if he were the one telling it, got up, pulled open a drawer, and reached way in the back. Among the tools in the drawer Horne spotted a pair of handcuffs. A small key protruded from one lock. She found what she was looking for. She held up two mis-shapened slugs.

"For the next two days his forehead was so hot you could fry an egg on it. It was three weeks before he was back on his feet. They paid him fourteen dollars and twenty-four cents for that one. He was on the job four years and never made more than five hundred a year, but of course he wasn't in it for the money. Hardly any of them were. When he was able to go back to work they sent him off with a bunch after a half-breed, John Yellow Hawk. Train robber, horse thief, whiskey peddler; bad, bad medicine. They picked up his trail near the north fork of Rabbit Creek just above the Texas border. He was expecting company. He'd built himself a log fort high on the rim of a cliff-sided canyon, and when the marshals showed up, he was ready.

"The shooting started at sunrise. Yellow Hawk had about ten other curly wolves with him. The marshals couldn't figure a safe way to scale the canyon to get to the fort; they finally turned a flat-bed wagon into a movable barricade. That night under cover of darkness they rolled it up as close to the fort as they could; then, just before dawn, they lobbed a half-dozen sticks of dynamite into the fort. Blew up Yellow Hawk, his friend Bloody Hand, and a bunch of others. But three or four escaped injury. While the marshals were inspecting the damage and counting the dead, the survivors circled 'round behind them and chopped down nearly half before the marshals could rally and return fire and wipe them out. Ephraim was killed, shot in the back of the head. He's buried out behind the barn. That was his wish." She chuckled. "He said when he died he didn't want to be buried with a bunch of strangers. You see, he was a shy one, Ephraim was. But a good marshal, dedicated. Always got his man. Almost always."

T.G. borrowed a couple things from her, including the handcuffs. It was 5:42 by her parlor clock when he rode away.

Sedan was much larger than Muddy Springs. Wellington was five times the size of Sedan. He had no address for Dysart, so he made the rounds of the stores inquiring. A boy hawking newspapers in front of the Free Library knew Dysart. He was a fat little rosy-cheeked eight-year-old, sporting his big brother's cap and knickers with patches at the knees.

"Upstairs over Brickmeyer's Bakery. Down to the corner and turn right. There's a big sign out front and it smells real good. The stairs to upstairs are on the far side. Want to buy a paper?"

"Give me fifty."

"Wow! Shucks, I ain't got but twenty-two left."

Horne handed him a dollar. "Keep them, enjoy them, and thanks for the information." On he rode, easily locating the bakery and hobbling his horse.

Mounting the stairs, he decided on the aggressive approach. He knocked and opened the door. He had conjured up a mental picture of Dysart as a small man in his fifties, about Kimbell's age, round-shouldered, pasty-faced and with glasses magnifying his overworked eyes. Perhaps an ill-kempt mustache. At sight of him he got the shock of his life. The man sitting at the worktable in vest and shirt-sleeves was approximately the size of two dock wallopers, supporting sidewalk-wide shoulders, the chest of a carnival strongman, hands capable of bending him double in the wrong direction, and a voice that came up from the bakery below.

"You can't wait vor me to open the door? Who are you? What you want?"

Horne took in the place at a glance. Opposite, an excellent reproduction of Rembrandt Peale's portrait of Washington graced the water-stained wall. Beneath it stretched a crude table littered with paint bottles and tubes, brushes, and a set of engraving tools neatly arrayed in a shallow wooden box. Documents and drawings, paintings, and a facsimile of the great seal of the Republic were pinned to the walls. The floor hadn't been swept in a year. He recognized the distinct odor of bay rum, so strong it overcame the pleasant smell of freshly baked bread wafting upward from the bakery below.

T.G. did not answer his questioner. Instead, he moved to the desk and pulled open a drawer. Dysart shot to his feet angrily and slammed it shut, but not before Horne espied the obverse plate of a one-hundred-dollar bill, Ben Franklin's bored expression centering it.

"Vot do you tink you're doing?"

"Dysart?"

"Vot you vant?"

"Is this usually the way you welcome new customers? So pleasantly?" He produced his deed to the Cockeyed Coyote, earlier removed from its frame. "How much to make an exact copy of this?" he set it in front of Dysart.

His reaction was precisely what Horne expected: initial shock followed by eruption of anxiety. He swept it to the floor with one hairy paw. "Get oud of here!"

Horne picked it up, put it back on the table before him, and held it in place. "What's the matter? You look upset. I'll give you twenty dollars to copy it. It shouldn't take long. And an easy job for a man with your enviable skills."

"Who the hell are you?"

"Hear from Addison lately?"

"I don't know nobody by dot name."

"Kimbell. Listen to me, Dysart. Your old friend from Carson City came to you and asked you to fake a deed and bill of sale for him. A deed just like this one, different name of course. I've seen both papers; you did a masterful job. You're good. I admire artistic talent. How much did he pay you? Or did you do it for free, for old times' sake?

"I didn't do nuttin' vor him."

"You do know him, your old cellmate. I know you do, so it's useless to lie to me. I'm not going to drag this out, Dysart. All I want is your cooperation." He restored the deed to his pocket. "I want you to admit you faked the papers for him. Write out a statement and sign it. I'll be your witness."

"I ain't writing nuttin'. Get oud of here or I trow you oud!" He got up slowly, towering over Horne threateningly. He could almost hear his muscles tighten. "You pull dot gun und I cham id down your troat."

"Sit down, Dysart."

Horne dug in his inside pocket and brought out Ephraim Tubbs' badge. On loan from Mary Alice. A six-pointed steel star with knobs on the points and the words "Deputy" and "Marshal" separated by the letters "U.S." Sight of the badge had exactly the effect he'd hoped for. Dysart's eyes jumped about in their sockets as if he were looking for a rathole to crawl into. Fear filled them, overflowing onto his face; his upper teeth found his lower lip and clamped it tightly. Then he let go of it and sighed softly.

"You just got out of prison. You did time for forgery. You came east, back home, and got right back into business. Can't keep a good man down, can you?"

"I didn' do nuttin', I'm clean."

"Don't waste your breath. I could send you right back. You could get a minimum of two years in Leavenworth for what you did for him, but I'll be honest with you. I don't want you, Dysart, I want him. And you're going to help me get him."

He had sat back down. His massive shoulders sagged in defeat. "I didn't do nuttin' bad, I never, just a favor vor a vriend."

"Of course. Out of loyalty. Commendable. Get a pen and ink and some paper. I want you to write what I dictate."

"Ja Ja, votever you say, I do id."

"That's more like it. You don't want to go back, I don't

want to send you. I mean, if you do go back it should be for something worthwhile, a successful counterfeiting operation or forging the *Mona Lisa*, not this piddling little rap."

"Ja ja." He examined the penpoint, wiped it with his thumb, and dipped it in the inkwell.

Ten minutes later, Dysart's sworn statement tucked safely in his pocket, leaving his hobbled horse under the stairs alongside the bakery, Horne set out for Judge Adrian Coombes' house on foot. He had left Dysart handcuffed to a steampipe just in case he took it into his head to skip town. Finding the judge was easier than locating Dysart; everybody in town knew His Honor. A bachelor, he lived in a small white house on a postage-stamp plot resplendent with a lush green lawn, shrubs, and flowers. His housekeeper answered Horne's knock. The judge was at the Elks Hall playing cards. It was getting dark by the time he got there. His route took him back past Brickmeyer's Bakery. Dysart upstairs studio was in darkness; Horne had deliberately left him in the dark to discourage any visitors.

He found the judge in a back room in the otherwise deserted hall playing dollar-limit poker with four friends. While the game went on T.G. told him of his encounter with Dysart and showed him his statement.

"That son of a bitch Kimbell," rasped the judge. "Devious scalawag. Congratulations, it looks like you're back in business. Of course I will have to have a word with this Dysart. It's always the same; they serve their time, they let 'em out, and they get right back into the business that got 'em into trouble in the first place."

"Can't teach an old dog new tricks, Adrian," said one of the others.

They had names, but Horne was so excited, while at the same time so relieved at the way things had turned out, he scarcely listened when the judge introduced them. Horne told him how he'd left Dysart.

"Good. Give him time to reflect on the wisdom of his predilection for a life of crime. Stupid idiot. Being a recidivist, he could get two years."

"I don't intend to press charges against him, Judge."

"What are you talking about?"

"He's the only man alive who could have nailed Kimbell for me, and he did. I owe him."

"How the hell did you get him to confess?" asked one of the others.

"He put the rope around his own neck," said another.

"How did you?" the judge asked.

Horne smiled. "Friendly persuasion."

Coombes cackled laughter. "I'll bet. I hope you didn't beat him up too bad."

"Never laid a hand on him. I didn't dare; he's a monster."

The man to the judge's left was dealing draw, putting His Honor under the gun, noted Horne.

"I'll go over there with you when we're done here. You don't mind waiting, do you?"

"Not at all. Enjoy yourself."

"He is," ventured the man sitting across from the judge. "He's winning everything in sight as usual."

"Care to sit in?" the dealer asked Horne.

Again Coombes laughed. "You don't want him in this game, Leon. The man's a pro. He'll shift the damned spots on the cards right under your nose." He paused. "On second thought, you wouldn't cheat a bunch of amateurs in a friendly game, would you?"

"I don't cheat, not unless forced to."

"Nobody'll force you in this game. Pull up a chair."

Horne took the first pot with jacks up and was congratulated all around. It was to be the friendliest of friendly games, he decided. The judge won the next two hands, the second with three kings. Horne watched him pull in the pot. He couldn't believe his eyes. He was tempted to pinch himself to see if he were dreaming.

The judge was cheating—flagrantly. Horne watched him brazenly, unhesitatingly cull all three kings from the previous discards, and while he distracted the others with a brief, wordy recapitulation of the surprising outcome of the trial, coolly drop the kings into his lap.

He showed no mercy; he seemed determined to win not most of the pots, but all. It was like a battle challenge that had to be met and overcome. Once in a while one of the others or Horne would sneak a pot away from him, but on average he took five out of six, and once eight in a row! Whatever honest instincts he harbored became helpless prey to his greed and deeply ingrained, almost morbid fear of losing. He palmed discards, he dealt from the bottom, glimpsed the bottom card when he dealt and when he cut, kept up a running patter to distract his opponents, peeked and shifted the cut.

Once he was dealing draw, completed the deal for the first round of betting, giving himself his last card, took one look at his hand, and clumsily dropped it, the cards falling every which way.

"Oh dear, will you look at that! Did you ever see such a bungling incompetent! I'm so sorry."

"Mixed deal," intoned the man opposite him.

"No harm done," said another, "betting hadn't started yet."

"Yeah, but I had," began a third.

"Mixed deal is right," said the fourth.

Horne groaned inwardly. The judge's chicanery seemed to be glaringly obvious only to him. He'd pulled five useless cards, a hand impossible to improve on. He wanted a second chance so he'd deliberately manhandled his cards. Continuing to apologize for his awkwardness, he reshuffled, the cards were recut, and he dealt a second time.

And won the pot with three little fives. Horne marveled at his audacity. On top of it, if he, Horne, remembered rightly, the hand the judge had fumbled away was the first one in the past hour that he'd dealt and failed to win. What, he wondered, was the matter with him? Was he getting tired?

Horne had never seen such towering gall in his life. The man had the conscience of an ax murderer, the nerve of a pickpocket, the guts of a cat burglar, the ethics of a child molester, a cast-iron belly and a heart sculptured in flint. He won and won and won, and to Horne's amazement, everyone else at the table congratulated him every time. Until the man who'd invited Horne to sit in took hesitant and somewhat timid exception to an outrageous coincidence in the judge's favor.

"Two hands running, both times you won with three aces," he complained. "The same three, and you were dealing."

"Ike," said the judge in a hurt tone, "are you accusing me of cheating?"

"Course he's not, Adrian," said another.

The others chorused agreement. Ike looked properly sheepish and dropped it.

In dollar-limit poker over the course of the ensuing two hours Coombes won more than three hundred dollars. Everyone else lost. Horne dropped thirty-two dollars. He was tempted to cheat both times when he and the judge came up against each other, but discretion prevailed. He had him on his side against Kimbell; he'd be out of his mind to alienate his advocacy in something so important for the satisfaction offered by something so unimportant.

The game broke up at 10:30. They walked back to Brickmeyer's together. The streets were all but deserted. Gas lamps lit every corner.

"Boy," sang the judge happily, "I sure had the luck of the devil tonight."

"You sure did, but of course you played your cards very astutely."

"You think so?"

"Definitely."

"How nice of you to say so. I do value your opinion."

"Oh, yes, no matter how good cards are if you don't play them right you can wind up losers."

"That's true. Can I ask you a personal question? Now, I don't want you to take offense. But you are a professional. Ahem, you . . . ah, didn't cheat, did you?"

"No."

"I'm glad. Though if you did, I failed to catch it, and I was watching you. I'm glad you didn't. We're all friends, it's just a friendly game. Win some, lose some, everybody enjoys themselves. No place for bad feelings. I do have to say, though, I was a little miffed with Ike Waterbury, the druggist. You know, that business about my pulling three aces twice in a row. Ike can be a sore loser at times. It was a relief when he didn't press it."

Horne said nothing. He couldn't think of anything appropriate. Coombes went on modestly crediting "the luck of the devil" for his success of the evening. They came within sight of the bakery. Horne started. An upstairs window showed light. He broke into a trot. The judge came pounding and puffing after him. They ascended the stairs two at a time. Horne pushed open the door. The light came from a small lamp atop the desk. The place was empty. Deputy U.S. Marshal Ephraim Tubbs' handcuffs lay open on the floor, beside them the bandana Horne had gagged Dysart with.

"How in the hell did he get the cuffs open? Thank God I've got his statement."

He turned to the judge. A strange expression had taken over his face.

"Yes . . ."

"Is something wrong?"

"I just wish we had him as well. I did want to talk to him."

"Isn't his sworn statement enough?"

"Well . . ."

"Will you please say what your thinking?"

"Take it easy, son, I just wish a third party witnessed it. Somebody with no ax to grind. Sworn statements can be obtained under duress, you know. That's why it's always good to discuss the thing face to face with the person who makes the statement. You understand."

"Are you saying you've changed your mind? I don't get the Coyote back? This is crazy!"

"Take it easy. We just have to go about things in acceptable legal fashion. The proper procedures. We can't cut corners. I can't. I took an oath to observe and uphold the law to the best of my ability, and every case that comes before me that's precisely what I do. I pride myself on my honesty and integrity."

On he raved, patting himself on the back. Horne's disappointment caught in his throat in a lump, blocking it slightly. But when he thought about it, he could hardly fault the judge. How can you fault a man for clinging to such lofty principles, a man who conducts himself so honestly, reputably, with such admirable integrity, even in something as relatively trivial as an insignificant card game among friends?

One thing was clear to Horne: Dysart hadn't freed himself. He'd either been expecting a visitor, or somebody had shown up unexpectedly, had found him, and picked the handcuff locks, probably his girlfriend.

When the judge was done polishing his image, he voiced one irrefutable point. Horne wouldn't have bothered to lock Dysart up and gag him for safekeeping if he didn't think His Honor wouldn't want to talk to him. So he really shouldn't complain over the importance the judge put on discussing Dysart's statement with him.

Horne took one last look around the studio, put out the lamp, and they descended the stairs. He was halfway down when he stopped short, turned about, and looked through the stairs behind and below and cursed.

"The son of a bitch took my horse!"

"So he has. Where, I wonder?"

Horne snapped his fingers. "To Muddy Springs. He must have. He probably had plenty of time to pack up before he got out, but as far as I can see, he didn't take a single thing with him. Which means he has no intention of leaving for good, at least not yet. He's gone to Muddy Springs to warn Kimbell."

"You seem very sure."

"I am. Have you got a horse?"

"I've got a buggy. I'll come with you."

16

It was nearing midnight by the time Horne and Judge Coombes arrived in Muddy Springs. Horne expected the Cockeyed Coyote and the other night spots in town to be carrying on full blast as usual. What he didn't expect was the large crowd milling about in front of the Coyote and his bay stallion with a large, familiar-looking body draped over the saddle. Light blazed from the entrance to the place. He could feel the excitement electrifying the sultry air. Marshal Bronkowski and his deputies were doing their best to break up the crowd. Roy Pendleton stood in the doorway in his apron.

The marshal recognized the judge and Horne and came over to them. Roy also approached with Eula-Mae and Francine-Mae.

"That's my horse," said Hornes, pointing to the bay. "I can prove it's mine by what's in the saddlebags."

"I believe you," said the marshal. "You know this fellow?" he turned Dysart's head so Horne could see his face.

"His name's Dysart. From Wellington. He's in cahoots with Kimbell. He stole my horse and rode over here to warn him the jig is up."

"What jig would that be? Never mind. Mr. Pendleton here can tell you what happened better than I."

Roy nodded. "He, Dysart, showed up about half an hour ago. Came bustin' into the place. Kimbell took one look at him and you could easy see they knew each other. Dysart was all flustered. Said he had to talk to him right away. They went into the casino. Kimbell's opened it up—not for gamblin', just for the tables where the customers can sit and chew the fat while they're drinkin'. The two of 'em walked through and out into the backyard. Francine-Mae here was servin' back there. Tell him what happened next, honey."

"I was bringing drinks to the table nearest the back door. I'd seen them go outside. The door was closed, so we couldn't hear them talking or anything. Then all of a sudden shooting started up. Everybody froze. Six shots. Then everybody jumped up and ran to the door. There was that fellow there lying facedown by the hitch rack. Bleeding like a stuck pig. Dead, you bet."

"And Kimbell?" Horne asked.

"Gone. We could hear his hoofbeats fading away."

"Son of a bitch!"

"The hitch rack out front was full up," said Roy. "Customers was hitchin' their mounts out back, you know. Kimbell grabbed the first one he could lay his hands on."

"Anybody see which way he rode off?"

"There's only one way from here for anybody on the run," said the marshal. "Down over the border into Indian territory."

A little sour-faced man came bustling up to Bronkowski. "Was my sorrel he stole, Marshal. You gonna get her back or what?"

"We'll try, Abner."

Abner made a face that said "Sure you will," and walked away muttering.

Horne turned to the judge. "Are you satisfied now Dysart was telling the truth in this statement?" He tapped his inside pocket containing the paper.

"I guess."

"You don't know?"

"You." The judge gestured to Roy Pendleton. "Kimbell's deed is in the safe, right?"

"Yes, sir."

"You know the combination?"

"I do."

"Go get it, I'd like to have a look. Let's have your deed, T.G."

Moments later, holding one in one hand, one in the other, he compared them.

"It's not the writing," he said to Horne, "or the contents, the wording, the date. It's the notary seal. The raised stamping on Dysart's version isn't as uniform as the real thing. Interesting . . ."

"What do you mean?"

"He could have saved himself work by bribing a notary to apply the genuine stamp."

"But if he did he'd be bringing in a third party. Kimbell might not have approved."

"That's so. Well, it looks to me like you win. I'll have to put my decision in writing, of course, for the record, but that's only a formality. Congratulations, T.G."

He shook ;his hand. Roy beamed. Eula-Mae and Francine-Mae cheered.

Horne glowed and just as quickly sobered. If only Star were here to celebrate. Kiowa country, he thought. And down through it deep into Indian territory, down to Texas.

"I'm going after him, Judge."

"Why bother? You got your place back, you're rid of him for good."

"I've still got a score to settle, a big one, the biggest."

"I think you'd be making a mistake. Let him go, good riddance to bad rubbish. The law'll catch up with him eventually. He'll get what's coming to him. You've got a job to do, a place of business to concentrate on. Are you listening?"

"Not really, Your Honor," piped Roy. "And I can't blame him. She sure was a pretty little thing."

"Sure was," said Eula-Mae and Francine-Mae together.

17

Perry joined them just in time to hear the judge deliver one last lecture to Horne on the questionable wisdom of chasing after Kimbell.

"It's witless, it's boneheaded. The law'll be after him, coming from sixteen different directions."

"He's right," said Bronkowski. "In three days there'll be wanted dodgers all over. He's wanted for murder, questioning in others, robbing that lady over in Sedan and throttling her. He's got enough on his head to hang him six times over."

"Are you listening, T.G.?" Perry asked.

"Yeah. Marshal, can I have my horse back?"

Dysart's body was draped over a deputy's horse and led away. Perry walked Horne to the stable, but it was locked for the night and in darkness. He left his horse in front of the hotel. Uncle and nephew went up to the room they shared.

"I don't care what anybody says," said Horne. "I'm getting a good night's sleep, and when I get up in the morning, I'm going after him."

"What's your plan? Are you going to ride around Indian territory dodging Kiowas and Comanches and beating the bushes the next four years? You'll love No Man's-Land. It makes the Mojave look like Paradise."

Each sat at the foot of his bed undressing. Perry scoffed, dismissing man, thinking and stubbornness with a single wave.

148

"I want him, Perry."

"So do a lot of others. Let me ask you this, if by some miracle on a par with the loaves and fishes feeding the multitude you do catch up with him, then what? What will you do, shoot it out? You've never shot to kill in your life. You carry around six pounds of hardware, putting on a big show for the yokels and your sense of self-preservation, but you never draw. I can't remember the last time you even cleaned one of your cannons. You're like every other professional gambler, all window display and no belly for gunplay. Why can't you be honest with yourself for a change? If you did get him in your sights, got the drop on him, you couldn't shoot him. You'd hesitate and he'd shoot you. T.G., leave him to the law.

"Besides, look in the mirror, you're exhausted. I've seen shadows with more energy. For days now you've been practically living in the saddle. Riding all over the landscape, charged with murder, gone through a nerve-racking trial, been pushed from pillar to post, pushed yourself until you're half-dead."

On he preached—earnestly, noted Horne, not lecturing him. His tone was one of appeal. In everything he said, in his every argument he was asking him to consider the thing objectively, sensibly, put aside his emotions. He acknowledged his manhood's right to exact vengeance for Star's brutal murder, but he practically entreated him to recognize the rashness of even attempting to act on his own. Risking his own life to avenge her death would be playing right into Kimbell's hands.

Horne had to admit he was even more impressed by his sincerity than his arguments. As to them, he could think of nothing to say to refute even one.

"You want revenge," Perry went on. "You'll get it. When they catch him and haul him into court. Knowing what you know, after what he's done to you, you'll be in a position to practically slip the rope around his neck. You'll see him dead, T.G., without having to personally pull the trigger. Am I right or wrong?"

"Mmmmm . . ."

"I didn't hear."

"I just can't stop thinking about her. She's my whole case against him, not the Coyote or Albert, none of the others."

"What you feel is only natural. You want to climb up on your white charger, point your lance, confront the dragon, and slay him. Only natural and admirably noble, but reckless and totally unnecessary. Sleep on it, son, and when you wake up, think about it with a clear head, with rested brain cells. You'll agree, you're not right and everybody else wrong."

"I agree now, I guess."

"I guess' means you still have misgivings. Tomorrow morning you won't, you'll see.'

He *was* exhausted; he fell asleep before Perry did, which was unusual. A dream arrived. Star, clad in her kimono, came gliding toward him across a sun-drenched lawn. Behind her, light shafted through a grove of enormous trees, resembling a cathedral. She came to his outstretched arms; he embraced her; they kissed. Their lips touching was exhilarating; he caught fire; down through his body and into his extremities it raced. He could feel them rising from the grass, their arms still around each other. They rose and as one tilted almost to the horizontal; and in the wink of an eye, still holding their kiss, they were making love. He was deep into her, she writhed sensuously; she was panting, gasping, wilting, melting in his embrace. Away they drifted locked together, floating through space surrounded by bright-blue sky. Far below, the lawn shrunk ever smaller until it was a patch no longer large enough to cover the palm of his hand. And the treetops blended into a darker, round green spot.

He could hear banging. He sat up blinking, rubbing his eyes. White sunlight angled through the window, washing the bare floor. Someone was pounding the door.

"Wake up in there!"

"Who . . ."

"Fire! Fire!

"Oh my God."

Horne pushed Perry so hard he nearly rolled him out of bed. He too awoke. Horne had wrapped the sheet about him and was stumbling toward the door, shoving the bolt, jerking it open.

"Fire! bellowed the clerk.

Horne glanced up the hall and down. No smoke, no sound of crackling flames.

"Out the window, look!"

They ran to the window. By now Perry was on his feet, standing in his underwear, not yet fully awake, beset by confusion. Horne stared out the window. Black smoke billowed up from a great, wide tongue of flame. It was the Coyote and the buildings on either side. Most of the block was going up like a matchbox. Men rushed toward the blaze carrying sloshing buckets. The wind was boxing the compass in unpredictable gusts; the flames leapt in capricious fury; the smoke blotted out the sun. The men rushing up with the water might as well have stood by and spit for all the good their efforts achieved. A barrel and pump on wheels was trundled up, two men manning the pump handle while others directed the skinny hose, water shooting from the brass nozzle in a wide arc, falling into the smoke.

"Great Caesar's ghost," murmured Perry.

"Kimbell!"

The clerk gaped at Horne. "The Coyote's a goner, all them buildings are, will be soon. If the flames make it across the alley by Goulson's feed and grain, the dance hall'll catch, the the whole rest of the block."

They jumped into their clothes, ran down and out into the street. The energetic pumpers were rapidly emptying their barrel; the water issuing from the nozzle showed steadily diminishing pressure. The bucket brigade had given up. The men stood watching the blaze, backing away as the wind shifted, bringing smoke toward them. Gradually, as Horne, Perry, and the others stood watching, the smoke thinned, revealing the charred skeleton of the Cockeyed Coyote. As Horne looked on in wordless horror, the few timbers still upright toppled under their own weight, leaving a clear view of the backyard and the flatland stretching beyond all the way to the Flint Hills.

"Kimbell," murmured Horne. "Kimbell."

Poking through the rubble an hour later, they found only two recognizable objects: the safe, completely blackened and still hot to the touch, the door fused at the edges to the body of the safe proper; and the Cockeyed Coyote head as black as pitch.

Bronkowski approached.

"Tough luck, T.G. You get it back last night and lose it again this morning."

"Kimbell did it. He rode out, doubled back—"

"I'm sure, only we haven't found any evidence of arson—no rags, nothing. Did find one thing, nothing to do with the fire. Last night after you two boys left, I went over to the Sunflower Hotel and got the night clerk to let me in Kimbell's room. He left everything he owned, except his money. Probably wearing a money belt. I found what I wanted."

He showed Horne a photograph. A picture of Kimbell and Star, heads touching, smiling for the camera. Taken before Jeff Kelleher began making eyes at her, Horne reflected. She looked happy, looked fond of Kimbell. She looked beautiful.

"Good shot of him for his wanted poster. If you want to tear it in half and keep her picture, you're welcome to."

Horne shook his head, "I don't think so; thanks anyway." He started off.

"Where are you going?" Perry asked.

"Back to the hotel. Get my horse. It's been standing out all night, it must be hungry and thirsty."

"Then what?"

Six strides away from him, his back to him, Horne pretended he didn't hear.

"I said then what?"

T.G. had no need for her picture to remember what she looked like. Twenty years into the future her face would still be indelibly imprinted on the screen of his mind, her name would come to his lips in lonely moments, he would feel her beside him in bed at night.

After tending to his horse and packing essentials, he

rode away—without saying good-bye to Perry, avoiding a scene and a lecture.

Sighting a weather-worn sign, the two words Indian Territory crudely carved into it, he crossed the border. He followed the Chikaskia River for a couple miles, then veered away to the southwest toward Medford. Indian territory, also called The Nations, he knew was not one huge crazy quilt of reservations each touching the other. Hundreds, perhaps thousands of white men lived there, traded with the Indians, stole from them, fought with them, raised cattle, and ignored them or got along reasonably well with them. But the vast area also provided sanctuary for rustlers, robbers, murderers, and other lawbreakers. To the east lay Arkansas, to the south Texas, to the west New Mexico, beyond the so-called public land, a name bestowed by the U.S. government and all but wholly ignored in favor of the Panhandle or No-Man's-Land.

Just below the Kansas border Cheyenne and Osage held forth. To the west and below the Cheyenne were Arapaho, and below their hunting grounds, the Kiowas and Comanches. Near the center of the territory the Caddos ranged. Fort Gibson near the Arkansas border and Forts Sill and Arbuckle to the south represented the Army's presence.

No Man but God's Land, a narrow strip stretching from the confluence of Beaver Creek and Kiowa Creek to the New Mexico border, was favored by a majority of outlaws on the run. Horne was convinced that Kimbell would be heading there, steering clear of any settlement of size, knowing that by week's end his wanted poster would be plastered all over. And the ominous words "Dead or Alive" would follow "Wanted."

No Man but God's Land, land of the buffalo Indians, checkerboarded with the white man's cattle ranches and ideal country for runaways from justice. In spring and summer the wide sweeping prairies were carpeted with lovely green grass and wildflowers. Buffalo and deer grazed contentedly on the succulent grama and bluestem grasses. In that beautiful period of the year it was a land of quiet, purling streams and deep, swift rivers. There could be seen towering cliffs, craggy spurs, and deep-cut crevices.

In July and early August the waters dried up under the unabating assault of the sun, the prairie grasses turned brown and parched, and the land shriveled like a corpse in the merciless heat. Fiery winds withered every growing thing, and humans and animals perished of heat and thirst. Occasional storms brought hailstones the size of hen's eggs; oceans of rain fell, flooding the plain to a depth of several inches, and the wind was so violent it could bowl over a loaded covered wagon or a grown man flat where he stood. In winter great blizzards brought thirty-foot drifts, burying homes and stock in bone-chilling cold.

In this strip two hundred miles long by forty miles wide, vigilante justice prevailed, but the lawless were not discouraged. Time passing and the ongoing influx of peaceful emigrants would efface the area's sordid reputation.

Horne rode at a leisurely gait, sparing his horse, until the sun hung directly overhead, without meeting a soul, without even seeing a house . . . or an Indian. The farther he traveled the more second thoughts assailed him. He began to get the feeling that he was riding into the lion's den. He began to see Kimbell crouching behind every boulder, hiding in every ditch and crevice. He wished now he'd taken the time to get hold of a rifle. he could bet Kimbell had one. His kind was always prepared.

He followed the Arkansas River undulating westward, riding within sight of it in a straight line. He had no idea how far ahead the Panhandle began. No idea how he'd recognize it when it did, until he remembered that it was just west of the confluence of Kiowa and Beaver creeks.

That night he slept under the stars. It was freezing cold despite being late summer. He was colder than he should have been thanks to skipping two meals, starting out reckoning that he could buy food along the way. He slept with his hand on his .45, his finger curled around the trigger. His nervousness woke him up repeatedly, so that by sunup he was exhausted. He decided that two nights in a row trying to sleep under such conditions was out of the question.

He made it to tiny Dacoma around midday; he had covered, by his rough estimate, more than eighty miles since Muddy Springs. He stabled his horse, got a room in the only public overnight facility—the Cherokee Inn—took a bath, ate two steaks, and went to bed at four in the afternoon, too tired to wander about town inquiring about Kimbell.

This he did the next morning, describing him in detail. No one in town had seen him. He stocked up on groceries and other essentials, mounted up, and left town. He wondered if Kimbell had outsmarted him, had taken off south or even east toward Arkansas. Neither would be as safe as No-Man's-Land. There he could hunker down and sit out the winter in front of a roaring fire.

He did know how to make a fire.

Horne pictured Kimbell coming upon a little ranch house that struck his fancy, knocking at the door, touching the brim of his hat in greeting to whoever opened it, and gunning them down in cold blood. Burying them in the backyard or perhaps under the hay in the barn. Did he have friends in No-Man's-Land? Probably; it was possible he knew half the renegades roaming the area.

Did he think he was being followed? Was he looking back over his shoulder? Again probably. Nobody had to list for Kimbell the scores Horne had to settle. He wished he knew somebody in No-Man's-Land, a rancher, someplace he could stay and use as a base of operations. Dacoma shrank smaller and smaller behind him until it was a black dot on the horizon. In front of him rose rugged mountains that from a distance looked so steep as to be unscalable. But the closer he drew, the less severe the slopes became. Through them twisted the Cimarron River and on the opposite side of them lay Lucky Creek. The next stream after that would be Beaver Creek. Beaver he would follow, and when Kiowa Creek joined it, he would be able to look westward into No-Man's-Land. He patted his .45 in its holster and thought back to Perry's impassioned appeal to his good judgment in the room the night before. His uncle, friend, and mentor had been dead-right about one thing: he could handle a gun, could shoot reasonably straight, but at a fellow human being?

"Fellow human being? That's good, that is."

And yet the intensity of his hatred notwithstanding, could he shoot Kimbell when they came face to face?

Perry didn't think so. Did he himself? He wanted to; the question was, could he? The trouble was he had no way of knowing until the confrontation came.

Perry's disgust and the surly tone it used for a voice were only a cover for his worry. Paul Flanagan understood and did not take exception of his behavior. They sat in the lawyer's office sharing a pint of Fillmore's bourbon. It was early evening.

"The son of a bitch is a lamb going to the slaughter," growled Perry. "Kimbell wants him to chase him; he's out there waiting for him. He'll bushwack him, get the drop on him, tease and taunt him until he gets bored, then do away with him. I'll never see the son of a bitch alive again, the son of a bitch!"

"My gracious, the situation is certainly taking a toll on your vocabulary."

"Son of a bitch!"

"I heard you. Maybe you're worrying unnecessarily. I'd say T.G.'s chances of finding him, of either finding the other—I mean ever—have to be one in ten thousand."

"You're not listening; he doesn't have to find him; he won't; Kimbell will find him. By God in heaven, if I was twenty years younger . . ."

"You'd go after him and get your head blown off, too."

Perry eyed him with the look of a man who'd just been kicked by his best friend and wondered why. "I wish you hadn't said that."

"Sorry, all I'm trying to say is fretting about it won't help any."

"Do you believe in mental telepathy?"

"Hell, no."

"I was up most of last night, sitting on the edge of the bed, consciously willing him to turn around and come back. You think it's possible to put your thoughts into someone else's head over distance? Some pretty intelligent people believe it can be done. I once read an article about it. It's called thought transference."

"I know what's called; I also know it's hogwash."

"You should keep an open mind."

"Not so open my brain falls out. Even if it were possible, what makes you think he'd listen to you when he can't hear you any more than when he could?"

He may be having a change of heart about going after him. Maybe all he needs along about now is a little shove to push him back into common sense."

"You're grasping at straws."

"You're a big help."

"I'm trying to be objective; I should think you'd want to be, too."

"I do, I do, only where he's concerned my heart tends to rise above my head." Drink in hand, Perry got up to look out the window into the street. "Hey, there goes Bronkowski."

Out the door he sprinted and down to the sidewalk. He called after the marshal; Bronkowski was carrying a thick pile of wanted posters. He held them up for Perry's approval. Perry ran up to him.

"By God, it looks just like him," he blurted.

"It should, it's his picture. I'm starting to distribute them right away. They'll be on every train out of here for the next three days."

"Great! Maybe some lawman'll catch up with him before T.G. does."

Flanagan had come up behind them. "That's your best hope, Perry."

"That's my only hope."

18

That night Horne camped near the west bank of Kiowa Creek near where it joined Beaver Creek. He had purchased a small skillet in Dacoma and cooked himself beans in fatback. He made coffee. He'd neglected to buy sugar and it tasted bitter as gall, but he told himself he'd get used to it, and it did perk him up.

He was getting used to many things, and fast: the countless small sacrifices in terms of comfort every man on the trail must make. You didn't carry a tent to keep out rain and dust and arrest the wind. No mattress, no plunge bath; the creek was his washbasin and his mirror. A large sandstone outcropping provided shelter against a cold wind that rose and rustled the leafless cottonwoods. It was about nine o'clock. He decided to retire for the night, get a good sleep and an early start tomorrow. In the outcropping he found a crevice just wide enough to fit into in which he could sleep out of sight of anyone approaching, four-footed or two.

He finished eating and prepared his bed, using his saddlebags for a pillow. The midsummer sun had shriveled and freed the leaves of cottonwoods, distributing them over the previously fallen cotton tassels whitening the ground like snow. He crammed the crevice with leaves and tassels and lay down in princely comfort. The stars overhead were as sharp as blue-white diamonds and a half-moon poised on its bottom edge, polished and shining as if from its own light.

Kimbell came back to his thoughts. He was never away very long. This time he returned with her. Horne envisioned them standing together at the bar in the saloon in Tonkin. She looked afraid of him; he looked arrogant, domineering, as if he were displaying her for all his friends to see and admire. And envy him. The wind sang its dirge, scooping up leaves under from beneath the tree off to his left on the riverbank, setting them dancing, then dropping. A late-arriving gust that followed sent them tumbling into the creek.

Horne sighed, closed his eyes, and wished it was over. He wished he was escorting him back to Muddy Springs with his hands tied in front of him, a rope around his neck, and his insolent leer, the only expression of amusement he'd mastered, vanished from his face.

Once more the wind came up. He heard a click: sharp, but barely audible. Had the rising wind not died a second before, he would not have heard it at all.

"My, my, isn't it a small world." He swallowed and went rigid. "Imagine bumping into you way out here." He sat up, turned slowly, and looked upward. Standing above him, the black eye of his Winchester staring balefully down, was Kimbell. Holding the rifle on him, he came down from the ledge, walking around in front of him.

" 'Evening, Addison."

"Ahhh, that's the spirit. I do like your attitude, T.G., always have. That time you came into the Coyote after the trial, asking about your deed. The perfect gentleman. It's class like you brings out the best in me. So you finally found me, did you?"

He laughed at his little joke. Then he leaned over, snaked out Horne's .45, smashed it into uselessness against the rock, and tossed it away. He patted him down, found his Sharps, and held it up.

"What do you do with this thing, pot field mice?"

He threw it into the water and went through his pockets. He got out the dagger-mounted knuckle-duster. "My, my, my, you certainly are loaded for bear." It followed the derringer into the creek.

Horne looked past him across the creek to where he'd

hobbled his horse for the night. Then his glance drifted down the line past the trees, discovering the dark outline of Kimbell's horse, the one—he recalled—he'd stolen from the little sour—faced man who'd complained to Bronkowski. Abner was his name.

"You want to stand up for me, T.G.? Would you do that, please?"

"Why bother? You're only going to shoot and down I'll fall again."

"My, my, you are in a grand rush, aren't you? What makes you think I'm going to shoot you?"

"Have you something a little more creative in mind?"

"We'll see. On your feet." Horne rose wearily. "Turn around." He obeyed. Kimbell hammered him with the barrel of his rifle at the base of his neck where it joined his right shoulder, dropping him to his knees. He fell the rest of the way and rolled over. It hurt like blazes, stunning him as if he'd hit him on the head. Kimbell had whipped out a length of rawhide; he speedily and expertly tied his wrists behind his back.

"On your belly."

Horne again complied. He could hear Kimbell's heavy step as he walked away. He came into his line of sight in front of him, walking to his horse. Moments later he came back with a rope.

"I'm going to tie you cradle, T.G. You know what cradle is?"

Painful was what it was. Could be excruciating, sheer torture, depending on how tightly you were trussed. He lay on his stomach as Kimbell tied his ankles, then pulled his heels up over his back and wound the end of the rope around his neck. An invention of his own; cradle usually joined wrists and ankles only. Either way it was a tie the average man could only endure for an hour or two at most—a man in superb physical condition, perhaps a bit longer. Horne did not fit the latter category. The ride from Muddy Springs had been rough on him, forcing him to use muscles and belabor bones unaccustomed to over-work. Like every professional gambler he spent most of his time sitting and, when he wasn't sitting, standing; not on a horse. Nor tied cradle.

Kimbell turned him around on the pivot of his navel, facing him east across the creek.

"In about seven hours you'll begin to see the sky lighten, take on a grayish-white hue. When the sun shows above the ridge, I want you to take a good long look at it. Admire it, enjoy it. It'll be the last time you ever see it."

"Why don't you just shoot?"

"Maybe I won't have to. In about an hour or so you'll probably pass out. If you don't strangle yourself to death. Who knows, maybe your heart'll give out."

"Sadistic bastard!"

Kimbell laughed. "You think this is sadistic? You want sadistic, I can show you sadistic. I've enough rope left over to cut eight or ten feet off and hang you from a lower limb of one of those trees. Hang you from your wrists. Then pile rocks on your back one by one until your spine snaps. That's sadistic. Let's talk about something else. Tell me something, how did you find me?" he laughed uproariously.

"You're a card, T.G. You're easier to read than McGuffey. When I left town the first time, I got about two miles out on the Braman road; I thought for sure you'd follow. I sat there three hours waiting. You disappointed me."

"Can you loosen my neck a little?"

"No. Don't interrupt. I had a lot of time to think about the situation and I decided that the marshal and your white-haired friend and Flanagan must have talked you out of following me. Or perhaps you were too tired. so I decided to go back; give you a second chance. I see it worked; burning down the Coyote was the straw that broke the camel's back, right? Speaking of broken backs. . ."

"Will you please shoot me!"

"Please? You've only been tied up four or five minutes. Grit your teeth, you'll be surprised how much pain you can stand if you really put your heart into it. You're a grown man, T.G., here's your chance to act like one, prove you're made of sterner stuff than you think. Than I think you are. Would you believe I wasn't more than half a mile behind you all the way from Muddy Springs? It's true, cross my heart. I was close enough to shoot you in the back a dozen times, fifty. But I don't shoot people in the back."

"You prefer to break their necks."

"If you mean her, I have to tell you that was an accident."

"Sure."

"It was. Oh, we got into a little argument, or should I say a big one? Over guess who . . . You've got to understand something about her. You didn't know her long enough, well enough to realize it, but she had a stubborn streak a mile wide. She really knew how to get under a man's skin. She's like every woman, she needed taming. Breaking. Like a horse. Of course you don't break a horse's spirit, or a dog's for that matter; what you do is tame them. Teach them to obey. That's all she needed, and time and again I thought I'd tamed her out there in Tonkin. But damned if she didn't turn on me when I'd least expect it. Sass me, disobey . . . You know yourself a woman should never do that to a man. Especially in front of others. It shames him, it's embarrassing.

"I tried every way I could think of to tame her. Once she got me so mad I hauled her up to my room with ten or eleven of my friends. Made her strip naked and give us all a good time. She ate and ate and ate. A woman'll do anything you tell her with a cocked gun to her head. I really figured that night would straighten her out permanently. From then on, when I said jump, she'd say how high. But then something happened."

"Kelleher."

"She told you about that? Was there anything personal between her and me she didn't tell you about?"

"She despised you."

"She tell you that? She's a liar; she was crazy about me."

"She was afraid of you. How can anyone love somebody they fear?"

"That was some wild night in that room."

"Why did you have to kill her?"

He already knew the answer to that: because she couldn't contain herself, couldn't resist downing Kimbell and praising him in comparison. Practically inviting him to murder her.

"You're not trying to tell me you miss her . . . That tramp? What was she? Nothing but a Georgia cracker whore—all tits and pussy. No heart, no feeling. Throw a dollar at her, snap your fingers, she'd fall on her back and spread her legs. Since she was twelve it's all she ever did: whore. Most women are born to be whores; it's all they can do, all they ever want to do. She was one: a white-trash whore."

The pain was gradually worsening; very soon now it would become intolerable; he would pass out. There'd be no need to shoot him. he'd strangle. The rope around his neck was already shrinking his windpipe so he had to fight to catch air. He gasped and gasped, struggling to get enough. His chest began to burn for lack of oxygen. So tightly were his wrists bound, the circulation was cut off. His fingers felt fat and lifeless. He was already a corpse from his nails down to his wrists.

Kimbell rambled on about her, criticizing her, villifying her. His words came straight from his inferiority complex, Horne knew. She had selected him in preference; her big mistake was in telling Kimbell.

"The day I bumped into her standing in front of the Coyote with the old gaffer, was I ever surprised! After all those years and more than a thousand miles from Tonkin. Amazing. I figured we could pick up where we left off. Of course, I didn't know at the time about you and her. Didn't even know she was working for you. How you doing?"

Horne didn't answer. Why bother? Whatever he said would only trigger a taunt. Kimbell really enjoyed this. He couldn't see his face, his leer, but his pleasure was in his tone. It wasn't even a half-hour yet and he was ready to give up the ghost. Be released from his agony. Why drag it out to its inevitable end?

He closed his eyes. He could hear the gentle movement of the creek, a soft, surging sound. He could see his horse across it, cropping the dead grass. He wished with all his heart he was dead.

His wishing heart was pounding so loudly he was surprised Kimbell didn't hear it and comment. He was beginning to drift into a half-sleep, propelled by his pain. He felt dazed, a beginning numbness. He nearly cried out in gratitude. Kimbell had crouched in front of him, studying his face, reading his agony with obvious satisfaction. Eye to eye they dueled in silence for perhaps two full minutes.

A sound came from behind his tormentor: hoofbeats. Kimbell heard and started to rise and turn, at the same time reaching for the rifle lying on the ground. A shot cracked, whistling over their heads. He was on his feet. Riders came galloping up, braking, waving rifles and six-guns at him. He need no order to drop his weapon. It clattered to rest and he raised his hands. A man had separated from the group and was over by his horse in the shadow of the trees. He freed its reins from the low branch Kimbell had tied it to and brought it over.

Horne stared. It was not Abner's blazed face sorrel stolen from behind the Coyote. It was a roan mare, a beautiful animal, its coat gleaming in the starlight. It swished its coal-black tail

"Get on the horse," growled the leader.

"Kimbell shrugged, grinned, and obeyed. In ten seconds they thundered away.

"Hey! What about me?" Horne yelled. "Hey!"

He strained his ears. Their hoofbeats grew fainter and fainter.

"Oh, my God, I don't believe it!"

All was silence for a long moment. He gave up, his heart surrendering to the inevitable. He began to will himself to die. Then out of the darkness came the sound of a single horse approaching. A boy no more than fifteen came barreling up, jumping down, the blade of the knife in his hand gleaming. He cut the rope connecting Horne's ankles and neck, then freed him completely. His hand found his throat.

"You okay?" the boy asked.

"I think my windpipe is cracked."

"It'll be okay, just don't swallow too hard."

Horne massaged it gingerly with the tips of his numbed fingers, then set about rubbing his wrists and ankles to restore the circulation.

"Who are you?" the boy asked.

"I've been following him from Kansas," Horne lied. What did he do to you and your friends? Don't tell me, stole a horse."

"Zeb Dankworth's. Outta his corral. He's just this side o' Kibby, about fifteen miles back. That thief left his own horse with a throwed shoe. Zeb came bustin' into town on another; we was all just sitting aroun' chewin' the fat. We took off after him, but lost his trail. Took us a couple hours to get back on it. Tracked him to here. . ."

"Thank God."

"He must be some mean son of a bitch to tie a man up like he tied you. Musta been torture."

"In spades. I won't ask what you intend to do with him."

"Hang him. Run him back to Zeb's place and string him from the bale-lifter. Come back with me. You can watch. It'll do your heart good."

Taking his time, pausing every time pain lanced a joint, Horne finally got to his feet and was able to stand erect.

"Think you can sit a horse?" the boy asked.

"I'm going to try. What's your name?"

"Addison." Horne froze. "Addison Quales. Somethin' wrong?"

"No. My name is Horne, Addison."

"Glad to meetcha, Mr. Horne."

"Not half as glad as I am to be able to meet you. Would you mind getting my horse for me?"

They rode at full gallop, trying to catch up with the others. Everything hurt. Every part, every inch. The small of his back felt like it had been struck with a twelve-pound sledgehammer. It radiated pain in every direction, but he didn't dare ask the boy to slow the pace, didn't dare risk arriving to find it was all over.

"There's no law in Kibby?" he asked.

"No law anyplace 'round these parts. We keep law and order ourselves. It's the only way."

"Aren't you a little young for a necktie party?"

"Are you kiddin'? I've been to lots. Everybody turns out, even little kids. Paw says it's the best lesson a body can have, best way there is to keep a man on the straight and narrow. To see for hisself what happens to them that strays."

Horne nodded. He ignored his discomfort; his mind raced. They intended to hang Kimbell as soon as they got him back. He couldn't let them, couldn't lose him now that the tables were turned. Only, how could he stop them?

They came within sight of the ranch he remembered passing earlier in the day. Torches lit up the front of the barn, throwing enormous, eerie shadows against it. Kimbell was astride a horse under the hay pulley, not the roan he'd stolen. It was nowhere to be seen. His hands were behind his back; he was bareheaded. Thirty or forty people had assembled to watch the execution. Horne and the boy rode up to the edge of the crowd. Horned tried to dismount; seeing his difficulty, Addison helped him down.

"Who's in charge? Horne asked.

The boy indicated the man who had done the talking in Kimbell's capture. "Mr. Quales, Paw."

Horne gimped over to him, and the boy came up alongside.

"Paw, this here's Mr. Horne; he's the one was all tussed up back there like a Christmas turkey."

Quales grunted and nodded without looking at either of them. In the torchlight just the side of his left eye looked as hard as a nailhead.

"We have to talk, Quales," said Horne.

"After. We're busy right now."

"About this. That man is my prisoner."

"That man stole Zeb Dankworth's prize mare. Finest animal 'round. Stole her and practically run her into the ground. Now he's gettin' what's comin' to him."

"You can't hang him."

Quales turned his head and looked at him for the first time. Horne held up Ephraim Tubbs' badge. Quales stared at him, then lowered his eyes.

"Depitty U.S. marshal."

"He's wanted for murder back in Kansas," Horne went on. "My orders are to bring him in alive."

Others close by, including some of the men who'd assisted in the capture, were listening.

"U.S. marshal," said one, with something like worry in his voice.

"I don't care," said Quales, "Nobody does. You're welcome to take his body back to Kansas and hang him a secon' time if you've a mind. We get firs' crack."

"Failure to turn a prisoner over to a U.S. marshal is a federal offense, mister."

"Don' care if it is."

Horne looked at Kimbell. A man on horseback had come up beside him and was preparing to place the noose around his neck. Kimbell was looking straight at Horne, but his eyes said he didn't see him.

"You damned well better care," said Horne evenly. "Unless you want to go to prison for two years. That's what the last man got who interfered. Obstruction of justice is a serious offense."

"Harley," said a man, "maybe we better hold off a bit and talk this over."

"I say we should," said a tall, bearded man, "and it's my horse was stole."

"Nothin' to talk about, Zeb," said Quales stubbornly.

A woman had come forward. She looked like the boy. She pushed between Horne and Quales.

"What's the dee-lay, Harley? Who's this?"

Horne held up his badge. "Maybe you can talk sense to him, ma'am."

"It's a federal offense to hang a U.S. marshal's pris'ner," piped the man who'd interrupted them moments before.

"Harley!" burst the woman.

"Why don't you shut your big mouth, Wiley Maddox," rasped Quales.

An argument erupted involving the Quales, Dankworth, and the men closest to them. Horne tried and finally succeeded in quieting everyone down.

"You're breaking the law, Quales," he said sternly, "He's my prisoner in my custody. You can't take him from me, can't harm him in any way."

"He stole a horse! You hang horse thieves; evvybody knows that!"

"He's fleeing a murder back in Kansas. That takes precedence over anything he may have done here. Whatever he's done, under the law he's entitled to his day in court."

"You don't try horse thieves, you hang 'em!"

"If you persist in refusing to hand him over, you'll leave me no choice but to arrest you for obstructing me in my attempt to perform my duty."

"Harley," wailed Mrs. Quales.

"Paw!" cried the boy

"Shit," boomed Harley. "You got some gall, Marshal. My son here saves your bacon and you turn 'round and pull this—"

"Hand over the prisoner, Quales. Now!"

Harley hurled his arms up, cursed a blue streak, and stomped off, followed by his wife and some of his friends. But not his son. The other onlookers did not move; they seemed to be waiting for the next scene in the drama.

Horne called over Zeb Dankworth. "Would you get him down from the horse and bring him here?"

"Yes, sir."

Horne looked about him. "I want to buy a forty-four or -five, I'll pay top dollar."

"You won't find nobody to sell you any kind o' weepon, Marshal," said a man who barely came up to the boy's shoulder. "Guns is too valible 'round these parts, too hard to come by, too 'spensive to ship all the way out here."

Horne could see that Kimbell, being brought over to him by Dankworth, was taking all this in with an amused expression. Horne paid no attention to him.

"Anybody have a horse they'd be willing to sell?"

"Same goes for horseflesh," said the little man.

"You could double-ride him to Dacoma, Marshal," said another. "You may have better luck there."

Kimbell laughed. Horne glared at him.

"I could really use a gun," he persisted.

Everyone had drifted into the semicircle facing him. They looked at him with sympathetic eyes, but no one said a word. Until the boy spoke.

"You can have my jackknife, Marshal."

The crowd tittered. The boy resented the reaction, but said nothing and did not take his eyes off Horne. He proffered the knife.

"Thanks, Addison, but only if you let me reimburse you."

"Huh?"

"Pay you for it."

The boy shook his head and set his jaw stubbornly.

"Your name Addison, boy?" Kimbell asked. "That's my name."

"Time you changed your name, Addison," said a wag in the crowd.

"Show's over," said another man, "lets all go on home."

It was apparent to Horne that Harley Quales was practically the only one in the gathering who resented his intrusion, at least enough to protest. He could see him standing with his wife, talking with four other men, and now and then casting a resentful look in his direction. His little voice warned him to get out of there.

"Get on my horse, Kimbell."

His wrists still tied behind his back, Horne had to help him mount.

"Where to, Marshal?" he asked, smirking.

"Dacoma."

His smirk gave way to a frown. "It's getting on toward midnight; I could use some sleep."

"So could I," said Horne, and climbed up behind him. He leaned down, shook hands with Addison Quales, heeled the horse, waved, and off they rode.

19

They stopped for the night by Trader Creek. From what Horne could see, Kimbell appeared much less fatigued than he did, despite his continuous complaining about how exhausted he was. He should be fresher, since he hadn't been the one tied cradle. Horne still ached all over; both shoulders felt as if he so much as raised his elbow or carelessly twisted his upper arm, they would pop from their sockets.

They lay on their sides facing each other, about twelve feet separating them.

"I haven't eaten all day," said Kimbell wistfully, looking as hangdog as he could make himself.

"Tough."

"You've got food in your saddlebags. How about breaking some out?"

"Tomorrow morning."

"You can't treat me like this. You're supposed to treat prisoners like human beings. That's the law."

"Show me a human being and I'll treat him like one."

"The law. . ." He snickered. "You sure put one over on those yokels, but you can't fool me. Where'd you get that tin badge? Steal it? You're no more a U.S. marshal than that ugly kid back there. You've got no more authority than—"

"Shut up!"

"Shut me up. Threaten me with your pocket knife. Ha ha. You really are a card. Do you honestly think you can

get me back to Muddy Springs without a gun? With one
horse between us? Knowing you, you probably won't even
be able to find your way."

"I'll get you back. I'll get another horse and a gun in
Dacoma. We're only about forty miles from there. Three,
maybe four hours double-riding."

"That broken-down nag'll never make it, you'll see. I'm
thirsty."

Horne got out one of his canteens and held it to his lips,
then drank some himself. It was getting colder, he noted,
and the moon and stars were no longer visible. The air
had turned damp. If it intended to rain, he thought, let it
hold off until Dacoma. He checked Kimbell's wrist bindings.

"How do you expect me to sleep with my hands behind
my back? Can't you tie me in front?"

Horne bound his ankles with the reins, untied his wrists,
and began tying them in front.

"Not so tight," Kimbell complained.

"Don't push me, Kimbell; after what you did to me,
you're lucky I don't finish what Quales started. Keep in
mind, you're no more valuable to me alive than you are
dead."

"You can't kill me. You haven't the guts."

"You haven't the guts to try me."

He finished tying him, checked his efforts one last time
and moved away double the previous distance between
them, lying down under a cottonwood.

"What's the matter, worried I'll wriggle loose and sneak
up on you while you're asleep? Jump you? Better check
my bindings one last time . . ."

Horne didn't answer, didn't move. Propped on one
elbow, he scanned the overcast sky through the naked
branches. The creek moved so languidly, with so few
rocks to set it rippling, he could not even hear it. Kimbell
fell asleep and immediately began snoring. Horne watched
him; he thought about his wrist bindings. They were an
expert job, he assured himself, perfect.

He dozed but, despite his fatigue, could not drop off.
Now and then he would rise on one arm and look over at
the sleeping prisoner. On he snored, sleeping like an

innocent, his conscience either conveniently out of order or nonexistent, thought Horne ruefully.

He thought about tomorrow. He didn't like the idea of parading him through Dacoma for everyone to ogle and point at. Bargaining for a horse and some kind of weapon could drag out half the day. And the two of them would have to eat. Maybe Kimbell was right—he might never would get him back; maybe it just wasn't in the cards.

He slept fitfully, waking often, looking over at him, hating him a notch more each time, not just what he was, his crimes, but resenting his effect on him, the abuse to his nervous system, the stress of worrying about him.

He had closed his eyes and was drifting back into sleep, his aching body surrendering to it, when a sound reached his ears commanding his attention. He started to rise to look over at Kimbell who was up on his feet, rising from ridding his ankles of the reins binding them, rushing toward him. Swiftly closing the distance between them. Lunging the last few feet, throwing himself downward, his hands reaching to seize his throat.

Horne closed his right hand, tightening on the grip, swinging the Barns boot pistol upward, firing. The explosion was like a howitzer. The bullet hurtled straight into Kimbell's open mouth, driving through the roof of it, piercing the two protective membranes and the region laced with veins and arteries and cerebrospinal fluid, the third membrane, plowing through the soft, huge, pinkish-gray walnut of his brain, crashing through the helmet of his skull, emerging, arcing, dropping harmlessly into the creek.

Horne stood over him, the smoking Barns in his hand. He dropped it. The hole in the back of Kimbell's skull looked almost the size of a silver dollar. Gazing down at him, Horne felt a surging in his upper body, a peculiar glowing sensation.

Perry had been so wrong, he thought, saying T.G. couldn't shoot Kimbell, implying he hadn't the stomach for it. He had been wrong himself, agreeing at the time.

Horne walked past the body over to where Kimbell had lain. He retrieved the length of rawhide that had bound his wrists. He went back and picked up his Barns, restoring it to its leg holster. He had had only the one ball that came with it when he purchased it in Muddy Springs to replace the one taken from him on the night he and Perry were tarred and feathered a hundred years before.

Crouching beside Kimbell, he went through his pockets. He found not one wallet, but two, the contents of the second one identifying it as Dysart's. He also found a thick wad of fifty- and hundred-dollar bills in an envelope in his inside jacket pocket, what was left of Aveline Del Cassé's money.

He was pocketing Kimbell's wallet when something fell out of it: a picture of Star.

Horne buried Kimbell under the tree under which he had been lying, using a sharp rock to scoop out a shallow grave, and then slept peacefully and well the rest of the night. Early the next morning he made breakfast, then set out for Dacoma.

He felt rested, felt good. It surprised him. He would never have imagined he could shoot and kill another human being so easily, unhesitatingly, and without the slightest pang of conscience after the deed. On the contrary, he felt not only a sense of relief, but one of triumph. His conscience evidently approved. Star certainly would have, and so would the others.

Even Perry.